Dear Kristen,

You and I [share] tastes in the books we [love]. A writer doesn't always write like the authors he or she admires. I aspire to write

Evelyn
Marsh

as well, but only the readers (in this case you) can say if the writer has

S.W. Clemens

accomplished the goal and written something of worth.

I hope you enjoy getting to know Evelyn as much as I did.

Best Wishes,

Scott Clemens

This is a work of fiction. Any resemblance it bears to reality
is entirely coincidental.

ISBN 978-0-9966123-7-1

Also by S.W. Clemens

With Artistic License
Time Management: A Novel

Available from Amazon

For Evelyn, wherever you are

"Heaven has no rage like love to hatred turned,
Nor hell a fury like a woman scorned."
— William Congreve, *The Mourning Bride* (1697)

CHAPTER ONE

Evelyn's first murder was an accident.

She panicked. Her first thrust missed wide to the left, biting into earth. With the second she overcompensated and missed to the right. Then, as she drew back a third time, the poor creature froze, trembling with fear, staring straight at her, and Evelyn realized at the last moment that this was the wrong one, not the brazen patriarch with the malevolent eyes, but a smaller, timid, innocent creature. And then she struck. She didn't mean to do it. She would have taken it back if she could. It was as though her muscles, tensed and full of adrenaline were preprogrammed to act independently of her better self, overriding her intellect and moral reservations. The third thrust crushed the poor thing's back, and to her horror it didn't die quickly. Its mangled body twitched and squirmed. She thrust at it again and again, missing three times before delivering the coup de grâce. Then, realizing what she'd done, she fell to her knees.

The house on Via Sueños Perdidos, in whose front yard Evelyn knelt on this early spring morning, was one of those two-story Mediterranean-style affairs with cream-colored stucco, red-tiled roof and tiny balconies of wrought iron. It was built for a minor film actor whose star was already fading by the time the house was completed in the late 1940s. It was subsequently sold for back taxes and had been a bit of a white elephant for decades before her father bought it for her as a birthday present a month before her marriage.

"This is not a wedding present to the two of you," he'd emphasized. "Not that I'm saying your marriage won't last, though precious few do these days. I just want you to have something of your own, where you can work on your art without worrying about rent or mortgage payments."

She was thirty before she appreciated that she lived in a grander home than her parents. The house, its detached three-car garage and backyard were perched on a knoll, hidden from view by a profuse tangle of scrub oak that also obscured what could have been a panoramic view of the Pacific Ocean. Evelyn had lobbied to have the trees topped. Howard, her husband of twenty-five years, preferred the privacy the wild trees afforded.

Two great bougainvilleas adorned the façade, spreading a profusion of papery red flowers up either side of the entrance and spilling a bower over the front door. From the large black-and-white-marbled foyer, a staircase crooked its way upward, right, then left, and left again, up to the bedrooms and library on the second floor. On the right side of the foyer, between potted palms, a heavy, carved-oak door opened into Howard's study. To the left, an arched doorway let into the formal dining room. Straight ahead, a hallway led to a half bath on the right, the kitchen on the left, and the great room at the back with high trestlework ceilings, colorfully painted beams, and a large fireplace.

French doors let out onto the backyard where a small Spanish fountain stood in the shade of an ancient oak. Beyond, a narrow strip of lawn jigged to the left, rising to the highest point of the property where four forty-foot palm trees stood sentinel at the corners of the pool. At the far end, Evelyn kept a small herb garden at the foot of a purple-flowering jacaranda. From the lawn, the property dropped away toward the road below.

Briefcase in hand, Howard chose that moment to step out the front door. Seeing her in the flower bed on her knees, her head bent, with the morning light making a halo around the edge of her chestnut hair, he thought her the very picture of a Madonna, until she raised her shadowed face and he saw the desolation in her eyes. Then she burst into tears and covered her face with gloved hands, overcome with remorse.

"What is it? What's wrong?" he asked.

Through stifling tears, she admitted her guilt.

"That's good, isn't it? The little bastard's been plaguing your garden for weeks. I thought you wanted him gone."

"I just wanted him to go away. I didn't want to kill him. And this isn't the same one. You didn't see the way she looked at me."

"She? Oh, for Christ's sake, Evy!" he said in a tone of exasperation. "It was just a gopher. Don't be such a wimp!"

Her name was Evelyn, though Howard and his professional circle often called her Evy (rhymes with heavy). It was a nickname she'd always abhorred. If you had to shorten Evelyn, which was a perfectly fine name, why not Lynn, or Eve, or Eevee? Anything but Eh-vee. To turn the tables on him, when she was annoyed she called him Howie, but he didn't seem to mind the sobriquet.

She stood and, not wanting to show her tear-streaked face, turned away. "Could you bury her for me? Please?"

He looked at her sternly and shook his head in disapproval. Then he put his briefcase down on the stoop. "Let me have it." She handed him the shovel. He sunk the blade in the earth beside the marigolds.

"No, not there," Evelyn said, sniffling. "Over there by the roses."

He complied reluctantly. She didn't bother to explain her reasoning, but it had not been an arbitrary request. Despite her hatred of the patriarch of gophers, the fat one with the beady eyes who periodically stood up from his hole to glare defiantly at her, she would not bury one of his children where he might inadvertently find her while tunneling. That was a scene too cruel to contemplate.

Howard came back, scooped up the dead gopher, carried it to the hole he'd dug, and dropped it in. He took a shovelful of

3

dirt, and tipping it into the hole his knuckles brushed against the rosebush.

"Ow! Son of a bitch!" he swore, shaking his hand.

"You want my gloves?" she asked, holding up her gloved hands.

"They wouldn't fit," he grumbled, shoveling more dirt into the hole.

If the gloves don't fit, you must acquit, Evelyn thought ruefully.

"Ah, crap, I got blood on my shirt!"

Annoyed, Howard went back inside to change his shirt and bandage his fingers.

Evelyn dropped her gloves on the ground and followed him up to their bedroom. "Can I help?"

"You've done enough already," he scolded.

He went into the bathroom and began probing at the back of a finger with tweezers.

"I'm sorry about your fingers. Does it hurt?"

"Yes it hurts. What do you think?"

He pulled out the end of a thorn and wrapped Band Aids around two fingers. Then he changed shirts and grabbed his tie. "I'm late," he said, brushing by her.

She followed him downstairs and watched from the front walk. There was just enough room in front of the garage to turn a car around and head down the steep, narrow driveway.

She waved. He didn't look her way. She sighed, discouraged by the start to this day, and tried to put the poor gopher out of her mind.

CHAPTER TWO

Turning to go inside, she noticed Howard's briefcase left behind on the front stoop. She glanced down the drive. He was already out of sight. Hoping to catch him before he'd gone too far, she hurriedly punched his number into her cell phone. His phone's distinctive ring chimed from the briefcase.

Forty-five minutes later, she pulled to the curb in front of the law offices of Hightower, Marsden & Katz on East Figueroa. The building was a white three-story stucco affair with arched windows and red-tiled roof across from the City of Santa Barbara Police station and a couple of blocks from the County Superior Court. It had been a strategic location when her father, Bill Hightower, founded the firm with the expectation of capturing a walk-in clientele. Albert Katz had made a career of it, while Bill Hightower and Robert Marsden had lucked into a lucrative practice representing the burgeoning winery and vineyard businesses in nearby Santa Ynez Valley.

The founding partners had all retired. Albert Katz Jr., the second generation Katz at the firm, still practiced criminal law. Howard had naturally stepped into his father-in-law's shoes specializing in real estate law. Robert Marsden's children had taken different paths, and his place had been filled by Anthony Ball, an energetic, affable young man to whom Howard delegated the grunt work.

The receptionist, a pudgy young brunette with bright red lipstick, looked up inquiringly. "Can I help you?"

Evelyn smiled. "You must be new here."

"Excuse me?"

"I'm Evelyn Marsh."

"Oh! He's been on a conference call. I left a voice mail."

"I know," Evelyn said, holding up the briefcase.

"Would you like me to...?"

"No, I'll wait." She was hoping that bringing the briefcase might atone for the aggravation she'd caused him this morning.

"I'm Holly, by the way. I'm not that new actually. I've been here six months now."

"I don't come by as often as I used to," Evelyn explained, looking at the large painting on the wall behind Holly with a look of serene satisfaction.

A light went on in Holly's mind. "Oh, of course! You're the artist. It's beautiful."

"It's always been my favorite." Like most of her work, it was a still life that suggested the presence of someone who had only recently left the scene — a rocking chair on a porch overlooking the ocean; sandals carelessly kicked off; a half-drunk glass of iced tea on a small table; and a book, its pages fluttering in the breeze, left open on a porch railing.

Her father had placed it there nearly twenty years before, and in the ensuing years he'd hung her paintings in every office and corridor at the firm, in his own house, and in the homes of a good many of his friends. He'd been her biggest fan and, until recently, her only patron. "It was my first really large canvas."

"I've always liked the one in the conference room the best — the one on the beach with the towel and umbrella? I love the colors in that one."

Evelyn thanked her, and a moment later, Howard came around the corner. "Holly, did my...oh, good."

Evelyn smiled and handed him the briefcase.

"Thanks for being so prompt," he said, and kissed her warmly on the cheek, all apparently forgiven. "Did you meet Holly?"

"Yes, we've been chatting."

"I was just saying how much I admire your wife's pictures."

Howard gave Evelyn a one-handed hug around the waist. "She's had a lot of practice. It's her special hobby."

He always appeared more ingratiating in public, she thought, than in private.

6

"Thanks again for bringing…"

They were interrupted by Albert Katz Jr., who mockingly greeted her with his best mafioso impression. "How you doin', killer?" Evelyn was momentarily startled into silence. Then he laughed. "Or should I address you as Gopher Slayer?"

Evelyn felt like she'd been slapped. "That's not funny," she said. She glanced at Howard with a feeling of disappointment. It was a little humiliation, but a humiliation nonetheless. Too many of his anecdotes were shared at her expense.

"I'm sorry you're so tenderhearted," Katz said. "Are you seeing my ex anytime soon?"

"We're having lunch as a matter of fact," Evelyn said.

"Just a word of caution: don't believe a word she says; you can't trust her." Katz looked knowingly from Evelyn to Howard and back.

"Keep it civil, Al," Howard warned.

"Always, always." Katz turned his back on them to address Holly on a business matter.

"I've gotta get back to work," Howard said, pecking her cheek again. "Thanks for bringing the briefcase."

At times she felt as though Howard were two people, one the polite and loving husband she'd known most of her life, the other continually annoyed with everything she said and did. Not knowing which she'd encounter at any given moment was trying her patience.

On the drive home, Katz's flippant salutation echoed in her mind: "How you doin', killer?" He'd meant it facetiously, a pale attempt at humor.

Evelyn Marsh, a killer? Nothing could be more ludicrous. No one who knew her would believe it.

But she had seen that poor, trembling creature frozen in fear, entirely at her mercy. In that moment she had held the power of life and death, and she had failed to stay her hand. She was the angel of death, and nothing she could do or say could bring the dead back to life. Death was irrevocable.

CHAPTER THREE

She pulled into her driveway only to find the pool service pickup truck blocking her way. She backed up and parked on the street. Walking up the steep drive, feeling a slow burn in her thighs, and noting the necessity of having to take deep breaths, she resolved to get more exercise. It had hardly been necessary in her youth, but at forty-nine she was finding that she had to work harder to stay fit and firm.

She'd barely had time to fill a glass of water before Mario Beltramo knocked on the French doors. A short, leathery man in his midsixties, he wore shorts, sandals, a polo shirt, and a Foreign Legion hat to protect his bald head and neck.

"I'm sorry to have to tell you this, Mrs. Marsh, but I have to give you my two weeks' notice. I'm retiring. My wife had a stroke, and I need to stay home and take care of her."

"Oh my, I'm so sorry. That's terrible, terrible news. It must be serious."

"Yes, ma'am, it is. She's weak on the right side and has trouble walking and talking."

"Is she...Does she have speech therapy? Will physical therapy help?"

"The doctor says she might recover a little speech, with time, but...." He shrugged in resignation.

"Well, we'll be sorry to see you go. I can't imagine...You've been cleaning our pool since when? Since Samantha was a baby at least."

"Seventeen years."

"You've sold the business then?"

"No, ma'am, I'm just shuttin' her down. That's why I'm lettin' you know, so you have time to get somebody else."

"Do you have any recommendations?"

"Never kept much track of the competition; I was always busy enough. I'll leave you with a little advice though: you

8

wouldn't have to have your pool cleaned every week, if you just cut down that jacaranda. It's pretty, but it's a damned nuisance."

The Spindrift Hotel was the same pale pink as the first-day guests who lay roasting on the beach and lounging by the pool, the ones who would look like boiled lobsters by this time tomorrow. The pool fronted the beach, for there were always those who preferred the taste of chlorine to the taste of brine and seaweed.

Evelyn saw Connie Whitfield Katz and her young assistant Brooke Bass sitting in the shade of an umbrella on the upper patio. They might have been sisters. Both augmented blondes, they wore sun hats and sunglasses, and short dresses that showed plenty of décolletage, Connie in red, Brooke in black. They enveloped Evelyn in the warmth of camaraderie and welcoming smiles.

"You remember Brooke?" Connie said.

"Of course. Who's minding the store?"

"I closed for lunch. We don't get much business on Tuesdays anyway. How have you been?"

"Okay. Still adjusting to being empty nested," Evelyn said, then reconsidered. "Actually, I'm feeling rather useless." She turned to Brooke to explain. "My son graduated from Berkeley last year and works in LA, and my daughter transferred from City College to UCLA this year, so...."

"What's she majoring in?" Brooke asked.

"Biology. Premed. She wants to be an anesthesiologist."

"At least now you have more time to paint," Connie said.

"Well, that's one consolation. But there's not enough life in the house. It feels very isolating. I rarely get out. As a matter of fact, I had to deliver Howard's briefcase this morning, and it was the first time I'd been to the office since my father retired last year. By the way, I saw your ex."

"Which one?"

"Albert, of course."

"What does he have to say?"

"Nothing nice."

The waiter arrived with the menus. When they ordered a bottle of Riesling, he asked for Brooke's driver's license. He held it a long time, looking from the license to Brooke and back. "The picture doesn't do you justice. I wouldn't have thought you were a day over nineteen," he said with a wink.

Brooke smiled at the compliment as he walked away. "He's cute."

"You said you had something to tell me," Evelyn said, looking to Connie. "Have you sold another of my paintings?"

Connie was the proprietor of The Whitfield Gallery on State Street. "Not this month. It's a hard sell at that price point, if you're not well known. But I expect sales to pick up with the summer crowd."

"You can always lower the price, if you think that would help. I won't mind."

"Are you working on anything new?" Brooke asked.

"I'm always working on something."

"I know we haven't sold much, but I really love your work. I think it has great potential...that is, I don't mean to say your work is less than it could be. I mean to say that it has great *commercial* potential. I'm always amazed at the really good local artists who can't make a living with their art, and I think you can."

"Not that she has to," Connie commented.

It might have been an innocent remark, but there was something subtly snide in her tone, Evelyn thought.

"You don't know how blessed you are," Connie said and, turning to Brooke, added, "She has a life most of us would die for."

"It's true. I admit it," Evelyn said. "I have a very comfortable life. I think that's probably what's held me back. I've never had to sell my work. And I didn't think I had the time to give it a go until the kids went off to college. You know I don't work very fast. I'm afraid I'm a bit of a perfectionist, which is not always to my advantage."

"You don't have to work fast to be successful with your art," Connie said, giving Brooke her cue.

Brooke rested her ample bosom on the table as she leaned forward and began speaking in an excited, conspiratorial tone.

"I thought of you last weekend when I was up in Half Moon Bay and came across this store on Main Street."

She was interrupted by the arrival of the waiter with a bottle of wine in an ice bucket on a stand. He made a ritual of it, ceremoniously popping the cork and pouring a tiny bit into Brooke's glass. She tasted it and smiled up at him. Then he poured a few ounces into Connie's and Evelyn's glasses. Lastly, he poured an extra measure into Brooke's glass and set it before her with a flourish. He wrapped the neck of the bottle in a cloth napkin before placing it back in the ice. "Have you decided?" he asked, trying unsuccessfully to avoid looking at Brooke's cleavage.

When he'd left with their orders Brooke said, "I think he's angling for a big tip."

"I think he's angling for more than *that*," Connie said.

Brooke smiled with self-satisfaction, well aware of the effect she was having on the young man. "As I was saying," she continued, "I came across this store. It's not a gallery, per se, because it doesn't represent a lot of *different* artists. It's just the work of one artist, Monica Surtees, but instead of just original paintings, she also sells all different-sized giclée reproductions, some framed, some unframed, some on canvas, some laminated, some limited edition signed pieces. The same artwork is on everything from mugs and calendars, to notepads and coasters, refrigerator magnets, place mats, postcards, posters — you name it. She even has a tabletop book and a coloring book. It's a brilliant concept. You know how much time you spend on a painting? Now, instead of being paid once for all that work, you can be paid over and over and over. For years! And everything you sell is like an advertisement for the original painting and for your work in general. Every morning when so-and-so picks up a mug with your painting on it, she'll be reminded of you and your work."

"It really is quite brilliant," Connie said. "It's the wave of the future."

"And it wouldn't cost much to start the business," Brooke added.

"Don't you need a catalogue of work?" Evelyn asked. "You only have...what? Three of my paintings? And I have only a dozen or so at home."

"You have twenty years of work," Connie protested.

"But it doesn't belong to me. I gave most of them away."

"They're all within your reach," Connie said. "They're in the homes of friends and family. And you have I don't know how many at the law office. You only need to borrow them long enough to have them scanned. Everyone would be happy to help."

"How much do you think it would cost?"

"Not worth thinking about. You'd make back any investment in short order. What I propose is this: at The Whitfield Gallery, we'll continue to sell originals. We'll also sell limited edition, large format, signed prints. All the peripheral items, smaller prints, and accessories would be marketed at the Evelyn Marsh Gallery and Gift Shop, or whatever you want to call it. You could refer clients to us. We'd refer clients to you. We could even do cross promotions."

"Wow," Evelyn said, "that's a lot to consider. You think it would work?"

"Positively."

After they'd eaten, Brooke left to reopen the gallery, while Connie and Evelyn lingered over their wine. The waiter came with the check and took Connie's credit card with a, "Thank you, ma'am, I'll be right back."

Connie raised an eyebrow at his retreating back. "Ma'am?" she scoffed. "I *hate* that."

"Well, he's just a boy. I expect we're invisible to him."

"He's not *that* young," Connie said indignantly, "and I'm not that old."

Evelyn restrained her tongue. She had never asked, but she thought Connie was around thirty-seven or thirty-eight. She'd become the trophy wife of Albert Katz a decade earlier, the ex-Mrs. Katz five years later, and she still judged herself by the reaction she drew from men.

Evelyn hated to acknowledge it, but she'd felt her own self-worth slip a notch or two as her youth faded. Menopause was as hard on self-esteem as on libido. She'd been told she was still a good-looking woman, but now that compliment might come, verbally or implied, with the qualification "for your age." With each passing year, it took more effort to look her best, and she would never again regain that inner glow and purity of skin that young women took for granted.

"He was practically drooling over Brooke," Connie added resentfully.

Evelyn considered replying, "It comes to all of us sooner or later," but thought better of it. She'd seen the way men ogled Connie; she still had many good years ahead of her.

Evelyn sipped her wine looking down on the pool. "You have a pool, don't you? What pool service do you use? My guy's retiring."

Connie brightened at the question. "I use The Pool Boy."

"Which one?"

"No, that's the name of the company: The Pool Boy. And his name is Ramon." Her eyes grew mischievous and she smiled. "He's hot, dark, and gorgeous."

"Is he reasonable?"

"He's hot, dark, and gorgeous," Connie repeated. "You want The Pool Boy."

CHAPTER FOUR

Howard had interned one summer at Hightower, Marsden & Katz while studying for the bar, before Evelyn's junior year at UCSC. They'd each been drawn to the other by virtue of the contrast they represented to their respective peers. Evelyn's classmates were aspiring artists, impractical dreamers, iconoclasts, and idealists all, who preferred partying to studying, and who excused bad behavior as "artistic temperament." And even though she saw herself in her classmates, she knew they were unrealistic, childish, and unreliable, whereas Howard was mature and pragmatic like her father. Howard's classmates were ambitious, directed, practical, and accepting of the status quo. And even though he saw himself in his classmates, he knew they were self-serving and boring, whereas Evelyn was a joyous free spirit, spontaneous, and creative. He also appreciated her feminine form, and if he were honest with himself, he knew that marrying the boss's daughter was a good career move.

When they married, he was making a comfortable salary as an associate attorney, which left Evelyn free to pursue her art. Her paintings in the early days chronicled her daily life. Subjects included a playpen empty of all but abandoned toys; a trail of Cheerios leading down a dark hallway past a castoff doll to a patch of light spilling from an open door; and a boy's bedroom strewn with all of its appurtenances, with curtains billowing before an open window.

There was never a time when she stopped painting, though after a time, childcare occupied the majority of her day. Howard, of course, did very little around the house, as he was busy at work. It made sense from the standpoint of a division of labor that the burden of childrearing should fall on her shoulders. As a result, turning her art into a business had never been a priority. Besides, she had never been adept at marketing. So, in an era when a two-wage-earner family was the norm, and women were encouraged to work outside the home, she had unwittingly become a housewife like her mother. Not that she regretted it. Her children were her best creations.

She had given up on ever selling her paintings until Connie Katz had approached her a year earlier. Having seen the treasure trove of paintings that graced the walls of the law offices and Evelyn's own home, Connie had asked to represent her, and in the ensuing months had sold four paintings. Now Brooke had shown her how she could connect with a greater public, and the idea excited her.

She wanted to share her enthusiasm with Howard. Dinner was ready at six. At seven forty-five, she ate a few bites and put the rest in the refrigerator. Howard came at twenty past eight.

"I wish you'd told me you were working late again," she said. "I would have made a later dinner."

"I'm not hungry anyway," he sighed. He crossed the foyer to his office and set down his briefcase.

"Are you feeling all right?" She reached up to feel his forehead.

He feinted to the left and brushed her hand away. "What are you doing?"

"You don't have a fever?"

"No, why?"

"You look flushed. Your hair is damp."

"I stopped off at the gym on the way home."

"Good for you. I should join. We could work out together." She followed him down the hall.

"I don't think you'd like it," he sighed.

"Connie says they have a Pilates class for women."

"I wish you wouldn't hang out with that woman."

"She's my agent."

"She's my business partner's ex, for heaven's sake."

15

"I don't see what that's got to do with anything."

"It's awkward."

"Here, let me take your coat."

"Not now. Do you want a gin and tonic?"

"No, thanks. I only like gin and tonic on a hot summer's day."

Howard fixed himself a tall glass and proceeded to the living room, where he kicked off his shoes and flopped into an easy chair. "A client is flying into town the Saturday after next. I've invited him and his wife to dinner here," he said, wiggling his toes.

"You might have asked me first."

"This is an important client. He represents a conglomerate that's looking into acquiring vineyards and a winery. It's important to keep him happy."

"He'd be happier if we took him out to a restaurant. I'm not a gourmet cook."

"This is more personal. It's a proven fact that people do business with people in their same social set."

"What am I supposed to cook?"

"They're from Texas. Let's give them something local. Dungeness crab would be nice."

"Should I make crab enchiladas, crab cakes, or crab sandwiches?"

"I don't care. You're the cook. Figure it out."

She was momentarily put off by his curt tone. Early in their marriage he'd been attentive and courteous. Even when the first blush of marital bliss had faded, there had been mutual respect. They'd both been proud of how well ordered their lives had become, how well they'd handled the transition from newlyweds to parents. Later, however, Howard had begun to feel neglected and resentful of the children, and now that they were young adults and lived apart, he seemed unsure of what purpose his marriage held. She often found he was impatient with her through no fault of her own.

"Will they be bringing wine?" she asked.

"I don't know. I'll have a couple of bottles set aside in case he doesn't — maybe something from the vineyard they're looking at. Chardonnay and Pinot."

"Maybe we should tailor the meal to the wine then."

"Yes, that would be good." Howard sipped his drink. "And Evy?"

She tensed at the use of her nickname. "Hmmm?"

"I don't want a repeat of the last fiasco. These people are from Texas. They don't share your politics, so stick to something you know about."

Evelyn bristled. "What? I can't have an opinion?"

"It's business, Evy. It's not fun and games. These people pay our bills. It's not good business to insult them. Just make polite conversation. You can do that." He pointed the remote at the television, which came on in the middle of a sitcom, effectively dismissing her.

Yes, she could make polite conversation with complete strangers; she'd done it before. It was her concession to Howard for the sacrifices he made. She knew the routine. They would have drinks, then give them a house tour. Howard liked to show off her house, as he felt it proffered the mantle of "old money," of the noblesse oblige that came with wealth and privilege, and it established his place in the pecking order. If length of stay conferred ownership, he had a right to claim it as his own, and Evelyn herself had no problem with his referring to it as "our house," but it rankled to be told how to act and what to say in a home she owned free and clear. "I have no interest in discussing politics, but if it's thrown in my face I won't be silent. Besides, that last time had nothing to do with politics, and everything to do with common decency."

"You provoked him."

"*I* provoked *him*?" she asked incredulously.

"Now, Evy, don't be difficult; I don't ask that much of you. My clients pay our bills. The least you can do is be pleasant on the few occasions I bring them home."

"The man was a fascist *and* a racist."

"Sometimes I think you have the emotional maturity of a three-year-old."

His hectoring tone provoked her ire. If she'd had a drink in her hand, she thought, she might have thrown it at him at that moment. Instead she gazed at her reflection in the French doors and waited for her resentment to pass. She had planned to share her excitement about the possibility of opening a gift shop of her own work, but the argument had soured her on conversation.

She left him without another word and went upstairs to the library to make a list of all of her paintings that currently hung in her own home, in her parents' home, in the law offices, and in the homes of friends to whom she'd given gifts over the years. It was a remarkable body of work for one who had only recently sold her first painting. Then again, the issue had never been about the quality of her work, but the complete lack of commercialization.

CHAPTER FIVE

Howard was toweling off after his morning shower.

She sat on the end of the bed. "I had lunch with Connie and Brooke yesterday. Do you know Brooke?"

"No, who?"

"Brooke."

"No."

"She's Connie's assistant. Anyway, she had an interesting idea."

Howard dropped his towel on the floor. Evelyn explained the opportunity as Howard began dressing, only half his attention focused on her spiel. When she was finished, he smirked. "You shouldn't pay attention to what other people have to say."

"No, but doesn't this make sense? I think it could work."

"What do you know about business?"

"Nothing, but..."

"Exactly. That's what I'm saying. You don't have a business mentality. You're a creative type. Don't try to be what you're not. You'd hate it."

"I thought you'd be excited. I might not make much at first, but maybe enough to..."

"We don't need the money," he interrupted, selecting a tie.

"It's not all about money. It's...I just haven't had much to do since the kids left home. I thought this would give me a good excuse to get out of the house, share my work."

"Listen to yourself. Be realistic; you know nothing about business. It might sound easy, but you wouldn't even have time to paint. There's overhead. You'd have to set up a corporation, have insurance, pay rent, pay employees, get permits, stock inventory. Jesus, Evy, get real. You're not suited to business."

"Connie could help."

"You know what I think about Connie. The less you see of her the better."

She had never considered Howard to be unsupportive. He'd always praised her paintings, but it seemed he only accepted painting as her hobby. Since she'd begun selling her work, he'd become dismissive. Now he left her feeling deflated.

"I can't just sit around the house all day; it gets lonely."

She stared at a younger family that smiled back from the photo on her dresser. They stood frozen in time six years earlier at the top of Healy Pass in Ireland. She remembered it was a windy day. Howard was holding on to his cap; her hair was in her face. Teenage versions of Robert and Samantha, wearing sock hats, exchanged pleased expressions. She missed them. She missed them all.

"Maybe I should get another dog," she said, thinking of her Shih Tzu, Bella, who had died the previous autumn.

"If you get one, don't expect me to walk it. Dogs are goddamned poop machines."

She moved to the window and looked down on the Spanish fountain. There wasn't a cloud in the sky. It was a warm spring day and she thought it would be a good day to start a new painting in the plein-air tradition. The subject would dictate the medium. Her early work had been in oils, but for the past eight years she'd worked mostly in pastels and watercolors. Some artists had a hard time switching media, but she'd always enjoyed the challenge, and no matter her choice, the finished piece was always recognizably her own.

She offered to make breakfast.

"Cream of Wheat would be nice, thanks. And coffee."

She went downstairs to the quiet kitchen, remembering the pleasant bustle of mornings when she'd seen the children off to school. There'd always been lost items to be retrieved, discussions about what to wear, after school plans, admonitions not to forget homework assignments, and questions, always questions — "Mom, have you seen my shoes?" "Where's my backpack?" "What time is it?" "Can you drive me to...?" "Can I go to...?" "Tryouts are today — can you pick me up at four?"

It had been a chaotic but happy house, a house full of life.

That morning Howard and Evelyn ate together (a rarity these days) at the small table in the breakfast nook in the kitchen. She'd discovered, in the absence of children, they had little to talk about.

He perused the headlines of the newspaper. "Oh god, here they go again," he remarked. "Our tax money at work. This plan for high-speed rail will be antiquated technology by the time it's built. Who will..."

Before their children had flown the coop, there had always been plenty to talk about — school and schedules, ambitions and dreams, relationships and entertainments. What did old married couples talk about? What did her parents talk about?

"And where does that leave those of us on the coast?" Howard asked rhetorically. She realized guiltily that she'd tuned him out.

"Sam posted the funniest video on Facebook," she said, looking down at her phone to call up the web page. "Check this out." She held the phone out to him so he could see the dancing dog.

Howard put aside the paper and gulped lukewarm coffee. "I don't see what this fascination is with social media. You'd think she had better things to do with her time."

Evelyn put the phone down. "When did you become such a curmudgeon?"

"Who's a curmudgeon? I'm not a curmudgeon."

"Just listen to yourself. We used to have fun." She got up to clear the bowls. "At least I think we did." She put the bowls in the sink.

"Come here," he said. He reached out and pulled her onto his lap. "What's got into you?"

"You're so negative."

"Am I? I don't mean to be. I have a lot on my mind."

"Like what?"

"Business. You don't want to know."

"Maybe we could get away for the weekend, go up to Monterey."

"Not this weekend; I'm busy. Sam'll be home soon. She'll cheer you up." He patted her bottom as he pushed her off his lap. "I've gotta get going."

He paused to hug her at the door, more like his old self, she thought. Closing the door, she remembered him putting his briefcase in the office the evening before. She rushed to get it and was at the end of the walk by the time he'd backed his black BMW out of the garage. She opened the passenger door and put his briefcase on the seat. "You're a lifesaver!" he said appreciatively.

CHAPTER SIX

It was just an idiom — "You're a lifesaver" — and it shouldn't have meant much, but this simple praise filled her with a sense of well-being that, unfortunately, lasted but a moment, for walking back to the house she saw the shovel standing upright in the earth, and suddenly she didn't feel like a "lifesaver." That tiny, helpless creature had cowered before her, terrified eyes searching for mercy, and what had she seen? A murderer. Evelyn liked to think of herself as compassionate and benevolent, and yet, in this instance she had been neither. She couldn't undo what she had done. All she could do in penance was to offer heartfelt remorse and silently cede the flower beds to the family of the slain. Did they worry when she disappeared from the burrow? Did they mourn her absence? They lived in their dark world under the yard, minding their own business. How could they know that people placed more value on ornamental plants than on the lives of gophers?

Evelyn tidied the house while planning her next painting. It would be a small one, she thought, of a café table after a morning meal, after the customer had left, before the waiter had come to clean off the dishes and cup. The table was set for two, but only one side would be messy. The other side would be set with flatware and a cup turned upside down on its saucer, as though the customer had expected company that never arrived. The table would be at the railing of a terrace high above the ocean, the sort one might find on the Amalfi Coast. With or without a table umbrella, she couldn't say (yet). She would start sketching that afternoon.

First, she wanted to talk to her father. After their children reached school age, she'd met Howard for lunch one or two days a week, but as the firm became more successful, he'd had little time for leisurely lunches. At the same time, Bill Hightower was spending more time nurturing business relationships and less on the day-to-day drudge work. He began taking a day a week for lunch with his daughter, a tradition that had continued for a decade until his semiretirement the year before (he no longer came into work, but he remained a voting partner and received consulting fees). She called to invite him out to lunch.

"I miss our lunches together," she said.

"I do, too, sweetheart. You know, there's no reason we can't make a new tradition in my retirement."

There was a reason, however, a reason Evelyn didn't feel comfortable voicing, and that reason was her mother. Not that she didn't love her mother, but the woman could be trying. She was the ultimate worrywart, and having very little to worry about in her own life, she kept an eye on the news so she could worry about people half a world away. As Connie had said of Evelyn, she had a life 'most people would die for,' a life of luxury and privilege, and yet she complained and fretted constantly. It was a life that was wasted on her, in Evelyn's opinion.

"Where would you like to go?" Evelyn asked.

"There's a new place, pretty close to home, I've been meaning to try. Why don't you come here first?"

"Sounds like fun."

"Is there an occasion?"

"No, no occasion. I just miss you, and I could use your advice."

"Nothing wrong, I hope?"

"No, no, just an opportunity."

"You know, your mother might like to join us."

"Of course," Evelyn said, making an effort to sound happy about it. "How's she doing?"

"Ah, well, her hip is bothering her again."

24

"I think she uses it as an excuse not to exercise. You should encourage her to walk with you." In his midseventies, Bill Hightower walked two to three miles a day, weather permitting.

"I do. She comes with me sometimes."

"If it's really serious, she could get hip replacement surgery. I know people that's worked wonders for."

"I don't think it's that bad," her father said, and abruptly changed the subject. "What are my grandkids up to?"

"I'll tell you all about it over lunch."

"I heard from your Uncle David," he said, referring to his brother who had married a Malaysian girl and worked in Finance in Singapore. "We Skyped a couple of weeks ago. Apparently your cousin Ronnie has applied to schools over here and his mother isn't happy about it. You might have some insight about it. I'll fill you in when you get here."

The Hightowers lived in a modest 2,700-square-foot ranch-style beach house on Avenue Del Mar in Carpenteria. The familiar briny, iodine scent of seaweed baking on the sand greeted Evelyn as she got out of her white BMW, a scent she always associated with childhood. They'd moved in when Evelyn was thirteen. It was a tiny house in comparison with the grand estates that hemmed it in on either side. However, what it lacked in grandeur it more than made up for in location. The property fronted the beach and gave them an unobstructed view of the water.

She let herself in the front door and announced, "I'm home!" For despite living in her own home in Hope Ranch for the past twenty-five years, she still had an emotional connection to her parental home.

Her mother, Marjorie Hightower, came around the corner and gave her a warm hug. "It's so good to see you. It's ridiculous we should live so close and not see you for weeks! But the time slips away." They went into the kitchen. "Would you like something to drink? Juice? Coffee?"

"I'll wait for lunch."

"I often think about calling, and then the time gets away from me. How have you been? What have you been up to? Your father's just getting out of the shower. These days he sleeps in and lounges around the house in his robe until afternoon. You know, getting your husband back, after fifty years of his going off to work, is a bit of an adjustment. I hardly know who I'm married to anymore. Can you imagine your father sleeping in?"

"Well, at his age, he deserves a bit of rest."

"I can't get used to it. What brings you our way?"

"I have an opportunity, a business proposition."

"Your father is the one to talk to. He knows about these things." Marjorie looked up at the ceiling, finally at a loss for words, at least for a moment.

"I wanted to make a list of my paintings that you have here."

"Oh, well, uh…" Marjorie looked this way and that, waving her hands back and forth in a way that reminded Evelyn of hula dancers. "They're all over the place, and I think we have a few in storage. I'm not sure — you know you've given us so many."

"And each one better than the next," Bill Hightower announced, buttoning his shirt. "How have you been, sweetheart?" He leaned over to kiss his daughter's cheek.

"Good. I'm really good."

"So, what's this about your paintings?"

"Oh, I've been making a list to...um...figure out how many we might have."

"Is this what you wanted to talk about?"

"Well, partly...kind of...."

They walked from room to room, while Evelyn made notes on a scratch pad. There were small paintings and large, some in oil, some watercolors, some pastels, some mixed media. Many of which she'd forgotten about. It was like looking at old photographs. You might entirely forget about something until you saw a photograph, and then it all came back in exquisite detail. For most, she could remember where she'd painted them, how old her children had been, and the motivation behind each subject. A few, however, blurred in her memory, and these she only vaguely remembered having seen before, as though they'd been painted by someone else. They stood before one of her larger paintings that hung above the mantlepiece in the living room. It was one of her coatrack series, with two coats and two hats hung in such a way that it almost looked as though they were two people hugging.

"I hope they haven't been damaged by the salt air," Marjorie said. "I've heard that can be detrimental. You know, I've been worried about that. And you know the sea level is rising. It might be better to move them to higher ground. After all, we're right here on the beach. If the sea level rises, we could be underwater. And what about tsunamis? You saw what happened in Indonesia and Japan, and here we are, right on the water. Oh my god, I don't even want to think about it! We'd lose everything!"

"Don't worry about it, Mom. You'll be long gone before that happens."

Marjorie seemed appalled by the idea. "I'm not going anywhere soon!"

"No, of course not," Evelyn said. "I just mean that even if the climate is warming, it takes time for seas to rise. We probably won't live to see it."

"That's not very encouraging."

"It's not something to worry about. Nothing you can do will stop it. It's always changing, in any case. You know, ten thousand years ago, before the end of the last Ice Age, you could walk out to the Channel Islands."

"Well, that just goes to show you what I'm talking about."

Bill Hightower asked, "Why the sudden interest in your old paintings?"

"You know I've been selling a few."

"About time, too," her father said. "I've always thought your work was museum quality."

Evelyn explained what Brooke had found in Half Moon Bay, and how she could employ a similar strategy with her own work. "Only Howard doesn't think it's a good idea, and I'm torn."

"How so?"

"Well, it's not like I need the money. And I don't have any business experience. He thinks I'd spend so much time learning how to run a business that I wouldn't have time to paint."

Her father sighed. "He has a point, though not a very good one. It's not like you have to do this alone. I'd be there to help you through it. He could help, too."

"Connie said she'd help."

Bill Hightower rolled his eyes to the ceiling at the mention of Connie Katz. "Yes, well, I suppose she might know a thing or two, though I'd prefer not to count on her coming through."

"What's that supposed to mean?"

"Never mind. I just...."

"What?"

"I don't entirely trust her motives. She always looks out for number one."

"Don't we all?" Marjorie asked.

"Do we?" Bill replied with arched eyebrows.

There was an uncomfortable silence in the wake of his rhetorical question. Then Evelyn continued, "It's true we don't need the money. But I've really felt validated, in a way, since I've sold a few. It's one thing to hear friends and family compliment your work. It's another thing entirely to have a stranger buy it to hang on a wall. If a stranger likes it, then it's not about you; it's about the painting itself. It gives it value. I like sharing my work. It gives me pleasure to know that other people enjoy it."

"Perfectly understandable," Bill said. "But what has that got to do with all these paintings here? Do you want to put them up for sale?"

"No, oh no, I wouldn't take them back. They were gifts. No, what I'd like to do is scan them. Then we can make prints in all different sizes, put them on cups and plates, placemats and calendars."

"I think it's a marvelous idea," he said. "I'd be happy to help in any way I can."

"If you could contact the people you've given paintings to...."

"Most of our friends," her mother said.

"Ask them if I could borrow them for a time, to scan them."

"We should get them to sign a waiver," Bill Hightower said, "allowing you to sell reproductions of their paintings. I don't think anyone would sue, but you can never be too careful, and it's a grey area under the law."

"It would be nice if you gave them merchandize," Marjorie suggested, "that featured their particular paintings. I think they'd get a kick out of that."

"It's settled then," Evelyn said. "I'll do it."

CHAPTER SEVEN

Evelyn might have heard the doorbell if she hadn't been so absorbed in her work. She was sketching at the small wrought iron table by the fountain when a stranger came around the side of the house. She looked up, holding onto the brim of her sun hat as a gust threatened to snatch it off her head. She was alone and would have been frightened, but for the young man's appearance. He wore a white polo shirt with a turquoise collar, white cotton duck pants, and sandals. He appeared to be in his late twenties, was well groomed, and walked with a relaxed yet confident gait. When he saw her his face lit up with a smile as though he were genuinely glad to see her, and he raised his hand in greeting.

"Mrs. Marsh? I tried the doorbell. Then I thought I'd come around to scope out the yard. I'm Ramon. The Pool Boy?"

"Oh, yes, nice to meet you." She shook his hand when he offered it — he had a firm grip. He held her hand and eyes a moment longer than usual as she registered his thick, dark hair, swarthy complexion, and genial brown eyes framed by long feminine lashes. There was nothing feminine about his physique, however. She noted his torso and arms were firm without being muscle-bound, and felt for just a moment like a schoolgirl at an athletic event, appreciating lithe, well-muscled bodies.

"I always try to meet my customers before I start to work. It helps if I'm not anonymous."

She noticed the barest trace of an accent and, given the number of immigrants both legal and illegal, one might assume he hailed from Mexico. It was her observation that those who were bilingual rarely lost the accent of the mother tongue entirely, though if she were hearing him on the phone, without preconceived expectations, she would not have been able to place his origins — the lilt wasn't quite right for Mexico, and he looked more European than mestizo. "I want to make sure I meet your needs. If you have any questions, concerns, or complaints, I want you to feel free to call me." He handed her his business card.

She looked at it. Aqua print gave the particulars:

Ramon Esposito
The Pool Boy
Licensed, Insured
805-790-2801

A logo of a diver springing from a board adorned the side of the card.

She wondered if Esposito was Spanish or Italian.

"I can't imagine what I'd have a question about. I don't think I ever had a question for Mario for all the years he worked for us. I'm content, as long as you do your job."

"Some people are very particular about the amount of chlorine in a pool, or the water temperature. You might need the heater or filter repaired or replaced. Sometimes tiles fall off, or coping cracks. Whatever your needs, we do it all."

"By we, I assume you mean you have a crew?"

For the first time, he looked a little embarrassed. He averted his eyes and cleared his throat. "Actually, no. There's just me. But I do it all. Whatever you need."

The more he spoke, the more curious she became, until she finally overcame her reluctance and said, "I hope you don't mind my asking, but I'm usually very good at placing accents, and I can't quite place yours. Where are you from originally?"

"I grew up in Torrance."

Now it was Evelyn's turn to be embarrassed, and she blushed. "I'm sorry. I shouldn't have assumed."

"No, you're right. Spanish and Italian were my first languages. I was born in Argentina, of Italian descent."

"I don't think I've ever met anyone from Argentina."

"I don't remember it. My family came here when I was an infant."

"What does your father do?" She asked the question, both to satisfy her curiosity and to engage in pleasant banter, while in the back of her mind she heard her mother scolding her for fraternizing with the help.

"My father was with the Argentine consulate for a number of years. He now consults for companies doing business with South America."

"And your mother?"

"She was a housewife. She's passed away."

"I'm sorry," she said. It was the polite thing to say, but it always left an awkward silence in its wake. One could never be truly sorry for another's loss, unless one knew the people involved. She knew neither the mother nor the son, which, of course, Ramon was trying to remedy by introducing himself. She admired him for taking the initiative, for trying to make his business a little more personal. Her previous pool man, Mario, had come and gone so discreetly he might have been invisible. He'd been working for her for over a decade before she'd learned he had grown children.

"It was a long time ago. Cancer. And what do you and your husband do? No, wait! I can see you're an artist," he said, gesturing to the sketchbook.

"Yes, and my husband is an attorney."

"Criminal law?"

"No, Real Estate."

"Really?" he asked, perking up with genuine interest. "What firm is he with?"

"Hightower, Marsden & Katz. Have you heard of it?"

"No, I don't think so." He glanced away and hypnotically repeated, "Hightower, Marsden & Katz. Hightower, Marsden, & Katz," committing it to memory. "I should talk to him. I have some ideas — something he might be interested in."

EVELYN MARSH

Evelyn didn't think so; the firm didn't handle small clients, and she knew Howard wouldn't appreciate a referral that wasn't worth his time. So she tried to discourage him by saying, "I think he has his hands full. He deals mostly in vineyard and winery acquisitions."

"Real estate is where the money is. In my business, I see all sorts of properties, all sorts of opportunities."

She regretted the turn of conversation and tried to steer the conversation back to his pool business. "Do you have many clients?"

"If I had any more, I'd have to hire an assistant, and that would require buying another truck. The problem is you need money to make money."

"Shall I show you the pool?"

"Let's take a look." He offered a hand to help her to her feet. It seemed the most natural thing in the world. He bowed slightly and swept an arm outward, palm upturned, in a graceful gesture that silently conveyed the phrase, "After you." She caught the scent of coconut oil as she stood. He stuck his hands in his pockets and they strolled up the lawn toward the pool. She liked the spongy feel of the grass beneath her bare feet. "Hightower, Marsden & Katz," he said. "I'll give him a call. It's all about connections. The thing is to dream big. You can't get ahead if you don't dream big."

She said nothing. He was a handsome young man with that edge of urgency that often accompanies ambition. Howard had had that edge when he was young and hungry for success.

The lawn ran right up to the coping. He knelt at the shallow end and dipped a hand in. "Is your heater broken?"

"No, I just never turn it on until the summer. It saves on the gas bill."

"Is your gas bill high?"

"I don't think it's higher than average. It is what it is. But I do know it doubles when we heat the pool."

33

"You really should consider installing a solar heating system. It's not expensive, and it would pay for itself within in two or three years."

"I suppose you can recommend an installer?"

"I told you, we take care of all your needs."

"We?" she teased, smiling.

"I mean I." He flashed a slightly embarrassed smile back at her. It was a flirtatious look she hadn't seen in many years.

"We probably won't use the pool much this year."

"Why is that?"

"Oh, my son got a job in LA, and my daughter is going to Europe with her roommate this summer."

Ramon drew back with a look of incredulity. Then his expression softened as if he suddenly understood. "Your stepchildren?"

"No, *my* children."

The look returned. "No, no," he mocked, "you can't possibly be old enough to have grown children."

"I assure you I am," she said, flushed with pleasure. She knew it was just empty flattery, but she was human, and who among us is immune to a compliment?

"I can't believe it. You must have been a child bride."

He smiled, letting his eyes rake her from her ankles to her eyes. He held her gaze a moment before resuming his inspection of the pool. Evelyn's heart beat a little faster. He examined the coping, the heater, and the pump. "Have you ever considered a pool cover? It would help keep the heat in, and it would keep the jacaranda blossoms out."

"That's what Mario said — my last pool guy — but I don't like the aesthetic. A pool cover looks so industrial. Besides, how are you going to earn your money, if you have nothing to do?" She wouldn't admit it, but she actually liked the look of purple blossoms floating on the surface of the aqua pool.

They were looking at the water when Evelyn dropped down on her knees, her left hand gripping the edge of the coping and her right stretched out as far as she could manage without tumbling into the pool. "Help me."

"What is it?"

"A bee. It's still alive." Bees must not be able to see water, she thought, for they often flew into the pool and drowned. They could be saved if you got them out fast enough. Once they became waterlogged, they could never recover. This one was not yet beyond hope. Its wings buzzed energetically propelling it forward, but it wasn't strong enough to break the surface tension of the water that held it in place. "It's too far to reach. Keep me from falling in."

He knelt behind her and gently grasped her hips. She stretched out further, concentrating on the buzzing insect, yet suddenly aware of the feel of his hands on her body, the tips of his fingers wrapping around to the front of her thighs, his palms pressing in against the swell of her hips. She felt a tingling electric current surge through her center, and a low growl formed in the back of her throat. The bee climbed onto her finger. She pulled back. He loosened his hold. They stood. She didn't dare look him in the eye. Instead, she concentrated on the bee, carrying it to her herb garden under the jacaranda at the far end of the pool. She held her finger against the edge of a basil leaf, grateful to the bee for taking its own sweet time to crawl off her finger.

"Do you do that often?" he asked.

She looked up and knew he must have felt something, too, for this time he could not hold her gaze and looked away. "Whenever I can."

"You're not afraid of being stung?"

"They never sting me; they know I'm here to help, poor things."

"You're a very kind lady."

"I just can't stand watching anything suffer."

"Is there anything else I can do for you?"

It was such an open-ended question, so fraught with possibilities that she didn't know quite how to answer. Her heartbeat was still elevated and she began to feel foolish. She was nearly old enough to be his mother. "I can't think of anything."

A sudden gust of wind took her hat off. She grabbed for it and missed. Ramon's hand shot out in a blur and caught it as a frog catches a fly. A rain of purple blossoms fell around them and into the pool, landed on her shoulders, and caught in her hair. He handed her hat back.

"I'll be by next Tuesday to service the pool."

She gave him a tentative smile and put the hat back on her head. "Thanks for saving my hat."

"My pleasure. It was nice meeting you, Mrs. Marsh."

"Evelyn, please."

"Evelyn," he said smoothly, "what a lovely name."

He turned to go, then turned back, cocked his head and smiled. "Hightower, Marsden & Katz. What's your husband's name again?"

"Howard."

"Howard. Hightower, Marsden & Katz. I should talk to him. I could make it worth his while."

CHAPTER EIGHT

The scene kept flitting through her mind during the quieter moments of the following days, and at night as she lay waiting for sleep. She realized she'd been readjusting her self-perception since menopause set in, had begun to see herself as an older woman. It was only natural. But for a few moments with Ramon she had felt young and vibrant again. She remembered his laughing eyes, and the way his hands had held her hips. It was unsettling. She wondered if she could recapture that feeling, and if she even wanted to.

When was the last time she'd felt like that with Howard? When had she last felt, if not desired, desirable? Not that she was looking for an affair, or would ever fall for a line, or anything so stupid. Nevertheless, eliciting a look of interest from the opposite sex had given the first thirty-five years of her life a certain zing and, she hated to admit it, contributed to her sense of self-worth. She'd always taken it for granted because that was the way it had been since puberty. It was as natural as the beating of her heart or the drawing of breath. Why being pretty should have any value, she didn't know...but it did. It just did. Pretty babies were fussed over. Pretty girls had more friends and got more attention. Pretty young women had the pick of the best men. That was life, whether we intellectually thought it fair or not.

Physically, she thought she'd been at her prime in her midtwenties just before Robbie was born. Howard had been more attentive then, too. When had he begun to lose interest? Or was it disloyal to imagine he had? But of course he had. People didn't stay young forever. Infatuation grew into love, love into commitment, commitment into marriage, which led inevitably (she felt) to children and adult responsibilities. She wouldn't trade that away to feel youthful again. Besides, longing for lost youth was a fruitless exercise.

She knew she should be satisfied. As Connie Katz had commented, she had a life to die for, and in spite of Connie's relative youth and stunning good looks, she would not have traded places with her. In truth, Evelyn pitied her. Women who had never had children just didn't get it, couldn't understand the fierce bond that you had, the joy of watching your child discover life's pleasures for the first time. If she were honest, she'd have to admit that her love for Howard paled in comparison. She'd met a few women like Connie who thought of children as a burden, expensive to feed, clothe, and educate, an impediment to pursuing their own desires and ambitions. They thought children got in the way, that you put your life on hold for them. But Evelyn knew from experience that there was no stronger bond than the bond between a mother and her children. She would lay down her life for them. Everything else was just window dressing.

So she found it troubling, now that her children had flown the coop, that she faced the rest of her life staring across the table at Howard. They were a couple again, after twenty-two years of often rowdy company, but they weren't the same inseparable couple they'd been in their twenties. Somewhere along the way, without understanding how, they'd made that transition from youthful vitality to calm maturity. Marriage had become less about romance and more about the business of raising kids and running a household, of scheduling appointments and keeping budgets, her own desires subordinate to maintaining order. She'd almost forgotten how it was to feel carefree and relevant. Slowly, without realizing it was happening, they'd become quite different people. Each day, each new experience, each repetition, settled one atop the other in layers, like sediment, each impression subtly affecting the next. What would they do now? What would they talk about?

She'd always admired her husband, yet she wondered if she were single now and meeting him now for the first time, would she still be attracted to him? He was certainly good-looking — in some ways better looking than when they'd first met. It was one of life's inequities that men acquired a certain attraction in middle-age, a fine patina of confidence and self-possession. Men seemed more comfortable in their own skins as they aged. Women were always worrying about how others viewed them as they lost their looks. She wasn't yet old, and she was in reasonably good shape, though she was quite aware of the crow's feet at the corners of her eyes, and the hint of furrows across her brow. She saw her future in her mother's face, the crepey neck, the jowls, and the droop at the corner of her mouth that gave her mother's face the impression of continual disapproval. Sipping her morning coffee in the kitchen, Evelyn thought she would have to guard against giving up and slipping into old age prematurely. She hoped to age gracefully, without resorting to plastic surgery and makeup to create the illusion of youth.

And what of Howard? Did he still find her attractive? She had seen herself through Ramon's eyes, and he had made her feel...not young, exactly, but desirable. She wondered if Howard were single now and meeting her for the first time, would he be attracted to her? Would he be attracted to any woman her age? Could he even tear himself away from work long enough to cultivate a relationship?

They'd had a decent sex life for the first fifteen years of marriage, comfortable if not lusty, lacking that breathless passion of their courtship perhaps, but providing simultaneous orgasms that left them satiated for the four or five days between couplings. If he was less attentive now, she couldn't begrudge him his fading ardor. Sex had become routine, constrained by one's narrow preferences, dulled by repetition, no longer novel, no longer spontaneous. Over the past five years, the frequency of their couplings had dwindled from twice a week, to once a week, and finally to once a week on Sunday between 8:30 and 10:30 a.m. He seemed too preoccupied with work to notice, and she had allowed herself to think of it as a natural result of menopause on her account and decreased testosterone on his. He was certainly harder to arouse, and she had almost given up ever having an orgasm again (save for an occasional date with her vibrator). Mentally and physically, it seemed clear that if she wanted to recapture some of her youthful exuberance, they would have to reinvent their relationship.

CHAPTER NINE

"Have you made a decision about the menu?" Howard asked, over a morning coffee in the kitchen.

"The menu?"

"For the Naives." — He pronounced it *Naves*. "My client?"

"The Knaves? How awful."

"What?"

"What an awful name — Knave: Dishonest."

"Huh? Oh! No, they spell it N-a-i-v-e."

"As in naïve? Innocent, unsophisticated. It's almost as bad."

"The man can't help the name he's born with."

"I'd change it. I'd take my wife's name. Why would anyone go through life as the butt of a joke?"

"I'm sure he..."

"Like Butts, for instance, or Hooker."

"Have you..."

"Or Dick."

"...decided what you're making?"

"Or Seaman."

Howard crossed his arms and rolled his eyes. "Can we stay on topic for a change?"

"I thought you said you wanted crab."

"I think that would be nice. What else?"

"What if they don't like seafood?"

"I hadn't thought of that."

"Chicken is always safe. I'll make crab cakes and chicken fettuccini in a béchamel sauce."

After a minute more of haggling, the menu was decided and Howard said, "Where do you get crab?"

"The supermarket, of course. Where else?"

"I don't want to take chances. I'm going into work Saturday morning. I'll stop by the harbor on my way back and pick up fresh crab. That should give you plenty of time before they show up for dinner."

"What time is that?"

"Their flight arrives at four thirty. They need time to get settled into their hotel. I'll pick them up around six fifteen, be back here around six thirty. We'll visit, have drinks. So what do you think? Seven? Seven fifteen?"

It was, she thought despairingly, the conversation of a man and his secretary. That wasn't unusual, she knew. After all, most conversations were of the mundane sort; this wasn't a fairy tale. But today she found it depressing.

Howard was already gone before she awoke on Saturday. She ate, showered, and dressed, then drank her coffee in Howard's study while she checked Facebook for updates from Samantha and Robert, read the headlines, perused a couple of articles, put in an order for art supplies, and searched for information on companies that print calendars and postcards.

When she could procrastinate no longer, she set about getting ready to entertain. It was a measure of how empty the house had become that it took no time at all to tidy up, which served as a reminder of how she'd been barely able to keep ahead of the mess when her children were young. She was prepping for dinner when Howard came home and placed a package wrapped in butcher's paper in the kitchen sink.

"The crab," he said. "I'm going to take a shower and lie down before I pick up the Naives."

He was halfway up the stairs when Evelyn exclaimed, "They're live!"

"Of course they're live!" he shouted back. "I said I was picking up fresh crab."

"I thought you meant fresh cooked."

He didn't answer. She looked at the two scuttling things in her sink, their pincers held closed by large blue rubber bands. They held their arms wide in a defensive posture. She ran water over them and they shrunk back. Then she filled a large pot with water and placed it on the stove. She'd never cooked live crab before, and she seemed to remember reading that the humane way to kill them was to put them in cool water and slowly bring the temperature up to a boil. It was supposed to lull them to sleep. Or was that frogs? She wasn't sure.

She was used to seeing red crabs, which is to say "cooked" crabs. The carapace of these ten-legged ocean-going bugs was purple with tiny white spots. She eyed the creatures warily. They might not be able to use their pincers, but that didn't mean they couldn't scratch. With rubber gloves to protect her hands, she reached for the biggest one with the intention of grasping it from the back, which she reasoned would make it difficult for the thing to grab her. She took hold of it with her right hand and lifted it out, its arms and legs flailing like an out-of-control gyroscope, and plopped it into the water. She did the same with the smaller one and peered into the pot. They sat on the bottom blowing tiny bubbles. She put a lid on the pot and turned the burner to low.

Then she set about making the béchamel sauce. She'd melted half a stick of butter and was sweating the onions when the lid on the pot clattered to the floor. She jumped in fright. The larger of the two crabs was trying to crawl out, and it was making high mewling sounds as bubbles issued from its mouth. She snatched a wooden spoon and tried to push the crab back, but it held firmly onto the rim of the pot. She had to pry the front arms and legs loose. As it slid back into the water, she quickly stooped for the lid, slammed it back on top, and turned the heat up a notch. She held her hand on the lid for a minute while her heart raced. They were supposed to go to sleep peacefully.

The onions demanded her attention. She stirred them, added a tablespoon of flour, half a cup of cream and a teaspoon of sage. The lid to the pot wobbled, then fell with a crash to the floor. Both crabs now clung to the edge, mewling hideously. Evelyn turned the heat off her sauce, then picked the pot up and poured its contents into the sink. The crabs were very active now. She poured cool water on them until they quieted some. Then she put on her rubber gloves and transferred them to a plastic trash bag.

She went upstairs to tell Howard that she had an errand to run, but he was still in the shower, so she left a short note on the bed: "Gone to the market, back soon."

She carried the trash bag to the car and drove down the winding streets toward the sea. At the end of Luneta Drive, she walked out onto the sand and, at the edge of the water, opened the bag and spilled the crabs onto the wet sand. The smaller one landed on its back, and as it flailed she noticed the blue rubber bands still holding its claws shut, without which, she knew, it would be helpless to defend itself, unable to hunt, unable to eat. She took a moment to consider how to remove the bands without risking being pinched. She used the only tool at hand, the tip of her house key, to snag the rubber band, then lifted the crab off the sand and shook it until the rubber band popped off. She repeated the procedure, and when all the rubber bands were off, she retreated and watched until both crabs were swallowed by the incoming tide. Then she drove to the supermarket and bought a dozen crab cakes from the deli counter.

Howard was in his study when she returned. She went back to her work in the kitchen and finished her béchamel sauce. She was cutting the ends off asparagus spears when Howard came in.

"Where are my crabs?" he asked.

She smiled and gestured toward the crab cakes that lay arranged on a baking sheet ready for heating.

"They weren't here when you went out," he said with raised eyebrows. "Did you take them for a walk?"

She looked sheepishly away. "I couldn't do it," she said softly. "They kept knocking the top off the pot. They wanted to live."

"Don't we all? What did you do with them?"

44

"I put them back."

"Put them back where?"

"The ocean."

Howard sighed heavily and shook his head. "Oh, Evy, Evy, Evy. It's a wonder we don't starve. You know what your problem is? You're too kindhearted."

"I can't help it."

"What's the difference if you kill it, or you let someone else do it for you?"

She shrugged. "Don't make me feel any guiltier than I already do."

"You're a piece of work," he said, turning away. There was a time he might have uttered those same words with a hint of amusement or at least tolerance in his tone. Now, watching him return to his study, she sensed exasperation, if not outright disdain.

Lying in bed staring at the ceiling the next morning, she asked a forthright question. "Do you still love me?"

"Of course. Why would you even ask?"

"You didn't have to tell them about the crabs."

"Well, it got a good laugh."

"At my expense."

"You have to admit, it was funny."

She remembered tears of laughter streaming down Tammy Naive's cheeks. She'd stopped laughing just long enough to pat Evelyn patronizingly on the arm and say, "You'd get used to it if you lived in Texas, honey. We shoot anything that moves, and eat it before sundown."

Then Tucker Naive had praised his wife's prowess with a gun. "And she's a wiz at skinnin' animals."

The whole conversation had made her feel small.

CHAPTER TEN

By sunset the following Monday, Evelyn had given up waiting for Howard to come home for dinner and was sitting alone at the kitchen table with a plate of reheated enchiladas, when her phone chimed. She checked the screen. Robert had made a move in their ongoing chess game. She studied the board and made a countermove, then left him a note: "Missing you as always. Hope work is going well. Love, Mom :)" Robert was a good chess player and won most of their games, which was just fine with Evelyn. She only played because it made her feel more connected. He'd been a loving little boy, but from adolescence on he'd distanced himself from his parents. She had hoped he would grow out of it in time, though as a newly minted adult he remained aloof and tacitly critical.

Then she checked Facebook. Samantha had posted new photos of her roommate, as well as a few of Robert and his latest girlfriend taken at a restaurant in LA. She was happy that her children had a close relationship, even if she was sometimes jealous. As small children they'd been best buddies. It wasn't until Robert went away to college that Evelyn had finally been allowed into her daughter's confidence, a role she now savored.

Howard came home after dark.

"I'm in here," she called out on hearing the front door open. "There are cheese enchiladas and salad."

"I had Mexican for lunch."

"I would have made something else, if I'd known. You didn't answer my texts."

"I don't answer personal emails or texts when I'm working."

"You were at lunch."

"They're working lunches."

She wished there was a way to check where he was lunching. It would make planning so much simpler.

He poured himself a Scotch and water and rummaged through the refrigerator for leftovers.

Taking note of his brusque manner and lack of eye contact, she asked, "Is everything all right?"

"Yeah. No. I'm annoyed. Your father called this afternoon."

"What did he want?"

"You didn't ask him to call?"

"No, why?"

"He wanted to discuss your new business. I already told you what I thought of that. It's ridiculous, and I know when it doesn't work out it'll cost me time and money to put straight."

"Can we talk about it?"

"I've already had my say." Then he turned and walked out of the kitchen. "I'll be in the study," he called back over his shoulder.

They may as well have been living in separate houses, she thought.

In the morning, Evelyn knelt in her herb garden, pulling weeds. A trickle of sweat rolled down her back. It was going to be a warm day. The air was torpid. She thought of Howard and the emotional distance between them, of her children both an hour or more away, of Mary Kay Hubbard, a neighbor with whom she'd once been friendly but who had moved away, of her art, of the proposed gift shop, and finally of Ramon. It was this last thought that gave her pause. The day before, the gardeners had come to trim the hedges and mow the lawn. That meant this was the day for The Pool Boy. He could show up at any moment. She imagined him coming up behind her in her sweat-stained blouse. Not that he would be interested. Not that he would care one way or the other. She was old enough to be....

She remembered the way he'd looked at her, and the thought of appearing old in his eyes left her feeling almost desperate for his approval. It was silly, she knew, but she didn't want to be ignored, with the image of Howard still fresh in her mind as he turned his back and walked away as though her opinions, wishes, dreams weren't worth discussing.

She left her gardening and went inside. She took a tepid shower, and because it was a hot day, she put on a swimming suit. It would be good to swim in cool water today. She considered her options — a bikini might accentuate her middle-aged hips. She opted for a blue-green, one-piece bathing suit with a deeply scooped back, as flattering a suit as she could manage. She looked at herself approvingly in the full-length mirror and, almost as an afterthought, applied subtle blush and lipstick. Then she put on a straw sun hat and large sunglasses, and took a book out to the pool. She reclined on a chaise lounge at the far end of the pool under the jacaranda, where she read for half an hour before falling asleep.

"What are you reading?" Ramon asked.

She snapped awake, disoriented for a moment, and looked up. Today he wore a straw hat, the sort lifeguards sometimes wore, and sandals. "Hello," she said with a welcoming smile.

He returned her smile and put down a small, blue, zippered case with several webbed pockets on the outside. There was a half-pocket for his phone, for various tools, sunscreen, and a spray can. He unzipped the case, withdrew a chemical kit, and knelt at the edge of the pool. With a nod of his head and a flick of his eyes he reminded her — "The book?"

"Oh, it's an Agatha Christie."

"Which one?"

"*The Mysterious Affair at Styles.* It's..."

"The first Hercule Poirot."

"Yes, you've read it?"

"A long time ago. It always struck me unlikely that the little Belgian could deduce so much from so little."

"Well, if no one could figure it out, it wouldn't be much of a story, now would it?"

"I don't remember the details, but I do remember he makes outlandish assumptions that somehow turn out to be correct. You couldn't write a book like that today — not with forensics and DNA. They don't have to assume anymore. The physical evidence doesn't lie."

"No, I suppose not."

Ramon took a dropper and squeezed three drops of chemicals into a plastic beaker full of pool water, capped it, shook it, and held it up to assess the color.

"Do you read much?" she asked.

"Not much fiction anymore. Stephen King, Michael Connelly. Mostly I read books on macroeconomics and business. I have ideas."

Evelyn laid her book aside, took off her hat and sunglasses, and rolled onto her stomach. She closed her eyes and listened to Ramon moving about the pool, skimming jacaranda blossoms from the surface, testing the pump and the heater, cleaning the filter. He returned to the little blue case, she knew, because she heard him pull the zipper. She opened an eye and saw him looking at the screen on his phone. He smiled, and put it back in its half-pocket on the outside of the blue case, where it stuck up like a pack of cigarettes from a shirt pocket. She closed her eye.

"You're going to get burned," he said. "Would you like me to rub sunscreen on your back?"

"Would you?"

Evelyn kept her eyes closed and tried to relax in anticipation of his touch. She heard him pop the top of a tube, and squeeze lotion into the palm of his hand, and rub his hands together. Then he was rubbing oil up her spine. He had strong, but gentle hands, kneading her muscles just enough as he worked from the small of her back to the nape of her neck. She let out an involuntary groan. "You should change professions," she said.

"I was a massage therapist in the summers between school terms."

"Really? Where did you go to school?"

"San Diego State."

Evelyn rolled onto her side and looked into his warm brown eyes framed by those beautiful long lashes. "You went to college? I never...I mean, I guess I assumed...I always thought pool boys were laid-back surfers, or...." She caught herself before saying anything insulting. Instead, she said, "I mean, it's not an intellectually demanding job."

"It's a good business."

"Yes, of course."

"Lie back down."

She complied, rolling back onto her front as he squirted more lotion onto his hands and began massaging it down her calves to her ankles.

"Oh, god," she groaned happily, "that's heavenly." He moved on to her feet. She'd heard about acupressure points on the soles of feet, and now she believed it; she was flooded with a sense of contentment. "What did you study?"

"I have a degree in business administration with a minor in economics. That's why I started this business."

"You are an amazing young man."

"Thank you."

"I mean it. You're an entrepreneur." She rolled onto her back so she could look at him while they talked. "I'm thinking of going into business myself."

"But you're an artist."

He moistened his hands with more sunscreen and continued massaging her feet as she told him of Brooke's idea.

He worked the lotion between her toes, then moved up her shin to the back of her knee, then to the muscle a few inches above her knee. She felt a tingle shoot up her inner thighs, which made her stop in midsentence. She hadn't felt anything so...so intimate with Howard in...what was it? — A year or two surely. Ramon didn't seem to notice in the least.

He said, "I think that's a fabulous idea. Nobody else is doing that downtown; you'll be the first. You'll be ahead of the crowd."

He stopped massaging her feet then and put the cap back on the tube of sunscreen. "Oh, hold on," he said, scooting forward on his knees. "Close your eyes." He squeezed another dollop onto his fingertips and touched it to the tip of her nose, smoothing it up the bridge. She felt his fingertips lightly touching her temples, then his thumbs fanning out like wings across her forehead and under her eyes as though he were sculpting her from clay. She had to consciously stop herself from trembling. "I don't plan on cleaning pools forever. I have a dream of investing in rental properties in tropical resorts. With interest rates so low, it would be easy to get a loan now, and the rental receipts would pay for the loan. It's like free money. Once it's paid off, it'll be like owning a private bank that keeps paying dividends. That's why I want to talk to your husband — Howard. Hightower, Marsden & Katz. See, I remember."

"You should do it. Go for your dreams."

"The problem is you need money to make money. You can't get a loan unless you have money for the down payment, and if you have money for a down payment, you probably don't need the loan. It's a Catch 22."

"I'm sure you'll find a way."

Ramon sighed and his lips turned up in a slight smile. "You're a very nice lady, Evelyn Marsh." He got to his feet and picked up his pool kit.

"I feel like I owe you a tip."

"For what?"

"The massage."

"It was my pleasure."

"I enjoyed our conversation," she said.

51

"I did, too. Until next week," he said with a wink, then turned and walked away. She admired his lean, supple body, his narrow hips and broad shoulders, his easy grace as he strolled down the lawn, and felt a pang of regret at his leaving.

CHAPTER ELEVEN

A pang of regret and perhaps just a little thrill of desire. Howard hadn't touched her like that in years. Ramon had this magical way of making her feel young again. She tried to push the thought out of her mind. He was only a few years older than her son, for heaven's sake. But he had the poise of an older man, a calm demeanor and an ease of manner that came with confidence. She thought of Robert who, like most young men, was often impatient, particularly around older women who seemed to inspire extremes of agitation or indifference. Ramon, by contrast, seemed possessed of an old soul, comfortable in her company, self-assured, polite without being obsequious.

A warm breeze sprang up. She began reading again but soon gave it up, the novel's flaws having been revealed. Ramon was right — the natty Belgian made extraordinary leaps of logic that were unsupported by the evidence, and she was continually reminded of how modern forensics would make most of his deductions superfluous. Given the same characters and circumstances in a contemporary setting, it would certainly be more difficult to get away with the crime.

The sun had moved behind the jacaranda, throwing dappled shadows that danced in the breeze. She put down the book, her hat and sunglasses and stood at the edge of the deep end, her thoughts returning to Ramon and the feel of his hands. If she were twenty years younger...She wondered if he had a girlfriend. Surely he must, she thought, a young man as attractive as that. She felt a sudden twinge of envy, for whoever the young lady was, she must feel very lucky indeed.

Then she dove into the cool water and began swimming laps, alternating between breaststroke, sidestroke, and backstroke, reveling in the texture of the water against her skin, emptying her mind of everything but the tactile pleasure of moving through liquid, and the sound of her own breathing. She swam fifty lengths and, pleasantly exhausted, pulled herself from the pool.

It was as she was toweling off that she stopped and smiled as an inspiration for a new painting presented itself. She would paint the herb garden: the rows of herbs; gardening gloves next to a trowel; the shovel standing upright, topped with a gardening hat that sported a peach colored ribbon fluttering in the breeze (to relieve the static nature of the composition); an arching branch adorned with purple blossoms framing the upper edge, and a tree trunk framing the right. She would entitle it, *Tending Your Garden*, in reference to Voltaire's *Candide*.

The rest of that week she drew sketches, and finally painted a small study in watercolors, though she was still undecided on what medium she would use in the final painting she envisioned.

She hardly thought of Ramon at all, except for Sunday morning at 9:30 a.m.

She awoke early that day and went downstairs to make coffee. She filled a bowl with cubed pears and carried it back upstairs. Howard was still sleeping. She placed the bowl on his night table, then showered and dabbed perfume on strategic places before climbing back into bed. She may not have been thinking precisely of Ramon, but he had awakened something in her, and for the first time in a long time she pleasantly anticipated making love to her husband. It was eight, about the time he usually awoke. He was still snoring. Making love over the past three years had become a routine, an obligation that rarely ended in an orgasm for her, to the point that she'd been trying to hurry him along and get him off so she could keep an appointment with her favorite pulsating showerhead.

Sex had been easy when she was young, but then it was new and exciting, and Howard had been trim and eager. He was still handsome in a suit, but naked — was it disloyal to admit it? — he looked flaccid and a touch paunchy and, if one were to be honest, just a little past his prime. Weren't they both? She acknowledged that. It was what they signed up for when they got married — for better or for worse, for richer or for poorer, until death did they part. It had been better for a long time, and it had been rich beyond her expectations, and now they would grow old together. She was reconciled to that, but she didn't want to give in to old age before her time. Hell, she wasn't that old! She was just forty-nine. Sure, Hollywood actresses had a shelf life that expired at forty or forty-five, but in real life, your story continued. The three-act play expanded to become five or six or seven. The goal, though no one wanted to admit it when standing at the altar, was to live long, stay healthy, and age gracefully together, older but wiser, without giving up all the things that had made life worth living when you were twenty or twenty-five or thirty. The trick was to grow, to enjoy the process of aging, to embrace the best that each stage of life had to offer, the wisdom you gained, the perspective of time, and push aside the vapid, mundane nonsense that distracted one's focus from the things that really mattered.

Ramon had reminded her that she wasn't yet really very old. She was still desirable, and she was ready this morning to show Howard that their love life was not yet dead. She waited. He snored. She scooted closer to him. He rolled onto his side. She reached out and lightly stroked his thigh. He snorted and rolled onto his back. His breathing returned to normal. She playfully gripped his cock and was surprised to find it already hard and fat as a sausage. He came half-awake and fell back to sleep, but his cock remained at the ready. She went under the covers and kissed it.

"What the hell, Lori! What are you doing!?"

He was awake now. Evelyn came up from under the covers. "Lori?" she asked. Lori had been his previous secretary.

"What?"

"You called out Lori when I...." She squeezed with force.

"Ow! What the fuck!?"

"Why did you call out Lori's name?"

"How the hell should I know? I was sleeping, for god's sake! I was dreaming. I was at work. Ow, Jesus, that hurt. What did you do?"

"Never mind."

"What time is it?"

"Time for you to get up. I'm going downstairs. I'll be back in an hour," she said with obvious annoyance.

Howard's unconscious response to her tender ministrations had put her in a foul mood. She made an omelette and toast. It took a strong Irish coffee to put her in the mood again, but when he finally rolled atop her, at nine thirty, she was thinking of Ramon. She didn't have to fake it this time.

Fog lay thick on the hillside when she saw Howard off on Tuesday morning, his black BMW nearly swallowed by it, as he reached the end of the driveway and turned left onto Via Sueños Perdidos. Evelyn went back inside, still wrapped in her robe, and settled in front of Howard's desktop computer with a cup of coffee. She bought a swimming suit online from Orvis, and a striped cotton top from Lands' End. Then she checked their stock portfolio and lastly her children's Facebook pages.

By the time she was out of the shower, the fog had burned off, leaving the house in bright sunshine. The lawn glistened with dew, and accumulated moisture still dripped from the trees. From her bedroom window, she could see the fog through the tops of the trees, spreading out like a sea of whipped cream all the way to the horizon. It was very quiet, save for the warbling of a mockingbird, the cooing of turtledoves in the palm trees, and far away the lonely song of a meadowlark.

She dressed in khaki shorts, a halter top, and flip-flops, then went downstairs to eat sushi and cantaloupe for breakfast. She made a move in her chess game with Robert, paid a few bills, and when she could procrastinate no longer, she set up her portable easel and sketchpad by the herb garden. She'd penciled several studies on her sketchpad, each displaying a different combination of angles and composition. She'd created them all from her imagination. This morning she was observing the real scene and adding details to her sketches. A hummingbird flew in to inspect the jacaranda blossoms, and she added it to one of the sketches. She contemplated adding edible flowers to the scene, almost discarded the idea, and finally settled on a few nasturtiums in the background.

Then, remembering, she added a gopher hole as a personal tribute and reminder to herself that one should tend one's own garden with kindness. She thought, without a shred of facetiousness, that if she ever got to heaven she would have to apologize to that gopher. With the exception of mosquitos, which she viewed as a scourge upon the earth, she had never before killed another living thing on purpose, and her one indiscretion weighed on her mind.

Everything had happened so fast. She'd turned over a shovelful of earth, seen the gopher scrabbling in confusion on the surface, and afraid it would burrow back underground to eat her roots, she'd panicked. She'd struck without thinking.

Now pushing the image from her mind, she turned back to the pencil study of the garden. She narrowed her preference down to two sketches, and waited for the right light that would give the best shadows. When it came, she would take a photo for reference and sketch in the shadows on her pad.

She was concentrating on how to make the background interesting without being cluttered, when a voice spoke up behind her.

"A still life?"

Evelyn shrieked and dropped her pencil. She whirled around, heart hammering. "Jesus Christ! You scared me! Are you always so quiet?"

Ramon stepped back and held up both hands. Today he was hatless, dressed in canvas pants and T-shirt. "My apologies. I guess the grass...."

Evelyn took a deep breath, and bent to retrieve her pencil just as Ramon did the same. They bumped heads. Ramon grabbed her arms to steady her, looking with concern straight into her eyes. Then he released his grip and handed her the pencil. They both rubbed their foreheads.

Evelyn gave a little laugh. "You certainly know how to make an entrance. Aren't you early? I didn't expect you until the afternoon."

"Each house takes more or less time depending on whether I'm just doing maintenance or a project or a repair, and sometimes, like today, I do the houses in reverse order, just to keep things interesting."

She took a deep breath, feeling her heart slow to a more moderate pace. "Next time, call out."

"Will do."

She turned back to her easel. He went about his work testing the chlorine level, cleaning the trap, skimming the blossoms off the surface of the water, and checking the heater and filter motors. When he was done, he looked over her shoulder.

"What can be so interesting?" he asked.

"Hmm?"

"What are you looking for?"

"I don't know exactly. There's just something missing, and I was hoping to figure it out. It's getting better, see?" She flipped through the sketches. "These two are my favorites."

"Why not this one?" he asked, flipping back a page.

"It's too busy, too cluttered."

"Let me see your favorite again." He studied it, looked up to examine the garden, then back to the drawing. "Are these petals? I can't tell without the color."

"Yes. They lead the eye from the bottom right toward the center."

"How about this?"

Ramon pulled the green garden hose over to the garden and laid it on the ground. It wasn't perfect, but it was the right idea. Evelyn could imagine how she'd paint it snaking in from the middle left, a little water issuing from the hose and dampening the ground before it, evidence that her trademark missing person had exited the scene to turn it on. She sketched it in, stopping a couple of times to erase.

"There, that does it," she said with satisfaction. "What do you think?"

"It's good. I like it." He was behind her and reached over her shoulder to point. "But what's this gopher hole doing here? I don't see any gopher hole."

"Don't be so literal. It's a metaphor."

"For what?"

"The darkness beneath the surface of things."

He humphed in acknowledgment. "Your back is getting burned. Do you have sunscreen?"

"I left it in the house."

"I have some. In my business, you can't do without it."

He rummaged in his case and came out with a squeeze bottle. She turned her back to him and lifted the hair from the nape of her neck as he squirted lotion on her shoulders. She was proud of her still naturally dark hair, unlike her mother, whose hair had remained the same color for decades thanks to dyeing.

He smoothed the liquid out with the palms of his hands, then his strong fingers squeezed her shoulders.

"That feels good."

"You have a knot. Lie down and I'll work on it."

"You don't have to."

"I don't mind. It won't take long."

He was matter-of-fact about it, she thought. She might find massage an intimate experience, but to him it had been a job. So she lay on her stomach on the chaise lounge, thinking that in her fantasies this was where she lured the young man to her bed. There was a term for that kind of woman — *cougar*. Could she be a cougar? No, she thought, that was a term reserved for promiscuous women in their thirties who preyed on inexperienced men in their early twenties. She was far too old to be a cougar, not to mention married. She was invisible to young men. As attractive as she found Ramon, and as young as he made her feel, she had to admit that the attraction wasn't mutual. She would turn fifty in less than a year. Half a century. Besides, she could never betray Howard like that. But flirtation was fun.

He knelt beside her and carefully kneaded the knot above her right shoulder blade. It hurt, but in a good way. In a minute, he left her shoulders and squeezed sunscreen onto her back, working it into her skin. Her shorts were loose and his fingers slipped under the waistline as he massaged her lower back at the base of her spine. She held her breath. Then he moved back to the middle of her back above her kidneys and she relaxed.

"There," he said, "your back is done. Would you like me to do the back of your legs?"

"Could you do that thing you did last time — with my feet? If you don't mind, that is."

"I don't mind." He slipped off her flip-flops. "Did you finish that book?"

"No, you ruined it for me."

"I did? I'm sorry," he said sincerely as he massaged the arch of her left foot.

"Well, it's true what you said. To arrive at his conclusions, Poirot has to make assumptions that are insupportable by the evidence. For instance, how could anyone suspect that the murderer had successfully impersonated a woman to obtain poison? Who would do that?" Ramon moved on to her right foot. "Who could pull it off? I don't know of any men who could pass for a woman. Though it did make me wonder how someone might get away with murder today. Of course many do get away with it."

"I don't think it's possible. 'Big Brother is watching.'"

"That can't be true, or every murder would be solved."

He squeezed a line of sunscreen onto the insides of her knees and began smoothing it in. "Gang bangers get away with it because no one will talk to the cops and they provide each other with alibis. The rest of us would get caught."

"Why would we?"

"Because the police can track your every movement, for one thing. There are security cameras everywhere. I'll bet I was photographed twenty times on my way here."

"Aren't you being a little paranoid?"

"A lot of these estates have security cameras."

"We don't," she said, wondering if their house could be considered an estate.

"It doesn't matter; your phone tracks your every move. Have you ever gone online or on your phone and a pop-up asks if this application can use your current location? Or used your phone's GPS?"

"Yes."

"Then your phone has a record of where you've been."

Ramon's hands ran up the back of her right thigh to the bottom of her shorts, then slid back to her knee. "Oh, yeah," she purred softly as he pressed on her tight hamstrings. He switched to the left leg, up and back, up and back, more slowly now, up and back, and this time his fingers pushed up under her shorts, just a knuckle or two. She tensed. His hands slid back down. Another line of sunscreen, then his left hand ran up the outside of her thigh, while his right ran up the inside. This time his fingers went much deeper.

"That's enough of that!" she shouted, slapping his hands away.

He held them palms up in apology, but there was still a question in his eyes. "I'm sorry, I thought...I guess I misread...."

Evelyn scrambled to her feet. "Yes, you most certainly did!" She did her best to sound indignant, but the words sounded false even to *her* ears. He was right. She *had* given him signals. She just hadn't counted on him picking them up. It was just a fantasy after all. He was supposed to be professional, immune to her fading charms. She was horrified at herself for leading him on. It was one thing to fantasize, but it was a little creepy when your fantasies came to life.

"I'm going inside," she said. She strode barefoot down the grass toward the house, her heart racing, ears burning with embarrassment.

"I'm sorry!" Ramon shouted after her. "Evelyn? Mrs. Marsh?"

She dead bolted the French doors and ran upstairs. What had she been thinking? In her bedroom, she looked out on the yard. Ramon was walking grim-faced down the lawn carrying his kit, his eyes downcast. She pulled back from the window and caught sight of herself in the mirror. She didn't want to look at herself. She wanted to disappear.

CHAPTER TWELVE

She felt dirty. She took a shower, as if the water could wash humiliation down the drain. How could she have been so stupid? She stood under the water for a long time and, unable to relax, turned to the pulsating showerhead for release. Afterwards she dressed in long pants and a modest blouse.

She imagined Howard coming home, seeing guilt written all over her face, and guessing the rest. He would be disgusted. He would feel betrayed. Even if she had chickened out in the end, she had fantasized about it. Deep down inside she had wanted it, and Howard would be able to tell.

She had never cheated on him...well, only once, and that didn't count, she told herself, because it was before they were married and it hadn't been her fault anyway. Shortly after they'd started dating, while she was still attending UCSC, and Howard was just beginning his career as an Associate in her father's law firm, she'd begun a flirtation with Steve Mead, a boy in her sculpting class. Steve was her fallback position if Howard's ardor cooled, because even though there was some truth to the old saying that "absence makes the heart grow fonder," there was also some truth in the adage "out of sight, out of mind."

Steve had lived across the hall in the coed dorm at UCSC, and had begun hanging out in her dorm room after class and in the evenings. He was a good conversationalist. He also knew a lot more about some subjects than she, which had proved useful on more than one occasion. It was nice to have someone to talk to. But from the start, Steve was more physically demonstrative than Howard, always rubbing the small of her back, stroking her arm, and on occasion playfully copping a feel. It was all pretty innocent on her part. She never let him go too far.

It was after they'd gone to the movies (*When Harry Met Sally*, Evelyn seemed to remember) that they stopped for an ice cream, and she noticed he was looking at her with a new sparkle in his eyes.

"What?" she asked.

"You are so incredibly beautiful, I could look at you all day," he said.

They held hands on the way back to the car. It seemed natural. Then, there in the parking garage, before he opened the car door, he'd swung her around and kissed her. Lost in the moment, she'd kissed him back.

He was an exceptional kisser. In retrospect, she had to admit that was probably the moment that had sealed her fate. But that was a long time ago and she had been physically, if not mentally, loyal to Howard ever since their marriage.

The thought of Ramon looking dejected made her writhe with self-loathing. If she was once flattered by his attentions, the thought of it now made her feel tawdry. It wasn't his fault. She was culpable and would have to own up to it. But how could she face him again? She couldn't fire him. That would be too unfair.

That evening Howard came home at half past seven. "I made a special dinner for you," she said hopefully, fearful that he would see right through her. "How was your day?"

"Oh, the city has been driving me crazy. The Redevelopment Agency keeps insisting my client give in to all kinds of concessions, and I keep telling them we're not obligated to do any of it, but they just won't listen. I'm beat and I still have work to do."

"Come sit down." The dining room table was set for two, the lights turned low, and two candles shed a warm glow that reflected in the half-full wineglasses. "You sit down and have some wine and I'll bring your plate." She returned two minutes later with two plates of steak, twice-baked potatoes au gratin, and spring peas.

"What's the occasion?" Howard asked.

"No occasion. We don't talk much anymore. I thought it would be nice."

"I don't have much to say. You don't want to hear about my clients. They bore even me."

"Sam's coming home this weekend. Her last final is Friday."

"That's good; you'll have company."

"Not for long, she's off to Europe in two weeks."

"Is that what I'm working for?"

"It's not going to cost much. The Overstreets have an apartment in Paris."

"Who are the Overstreets?"

"Gail's parents."

"Who's Gail?"

"Her roommate. How could you forget her roommate?"

"I don't know; I've never met her. Whatever happened to Catherine what's-her-name?"

"Phelps. She moved out last quarter."

"Well, I can't keep track of everything."

They chatted amiably over dinner and another glass of wine. He smiled. "This was nice. Thanks. Now I have to get back to work."

As she cleaned up the dishes she marveled at how easy it was to hide her guilt. He hadn't suspected a thing.

Howard went to the office Saturday. "That's why they pay me the big bucks," he explained over Evelyn's objections.

Samantha arrived after noon. Evelyn helped her bring in boxes from the Ford Expedition that Howard had insisted on buying her ("It's a tank in an accident," he'd explained). There were boxes of books and clothes; shoes and towels; a laptop; a pillow; sheets and a bedspread. Samantha elected to leave the rest in the car — a printer; one of Evelyn's paintings; flatware and kitchen utensils; pots, pans, plates, bowls, glassware; and a mug emblazoned with the UCLA Bruins logo. "There's no sense in unpacking," she said. "When we get back from Paris, we'll be moving into our new apartment."

"Park your car in the garage when you're finished," Evelyn said; "you're blocking the drive."

Samantha stacked the boxes of books in the closet, while Evelyn carried dirty sheets and clothes to the laundry.

The washing machine was just filling with water when Evelyn heard Samantha scream. There was nothing to be alarmed about; it was only Sam's phobic squeal at the sight of a spider. Evelyn found her pressed into a corner, trembling with fear, looking disturbingly like the gopher she'd murdered.

"Kill it!" Samantha shouted, pointing. "Kill it!"

"I'm not going to kill it. It's just a poor, little house spider. Open your window." Evelyn liked spiders. They had a will to live, and a natural wariness of people that she understood. She coaxed the spider onto her hand, carried it carefully to the window, and dropped it out. "I wish you'd go to a phobia specialist. It can't be good going through life afraid of the smallest things."

"It's just spiders. I hate spiders. Eww! They give me the creeps!"

"People are far more dangerous than spiders."

After dinner, while Howard watched a baseball game, Evelyn gathered together Michelin maps of France and Switzerland, and a map of the Paris Metro.

"Maps are so old school," Samantha said. "I don't need paper maps; I have my phone."

"Humor me," Evelyn said. "You might forget to charge your phone."

They made up a list of things to take on the trip. The girls planned to use the Paris apartment as their base, and make side trips to Alsace, Zurich, and the Côte d'Azur.

"Post updates and photos on your Facebook page," Evelyn requested, "so I can follow along vicariously. I want to know where you are and what you're seeing."

"Wait a minute; let me have your phone," Samantha said. She tapped the screen. Her own phone beeped.

"What are you doing?"

"It's Friend Finder. It's one of the apps that comes with your phone." She handed it back. "Now I'll just press Yes. There, now we're 'friends.' You can follow me on your phone. Now I'll ask you."

Evelyn's phone beeped. The app asked if she would like to share her location with Samantha Marsh. Evelyn tapped Yes. "Ah! Look at that!" she exclaimed, as a map appeared showing their precise location. "I had no idea this was on my phone." A snippet of conversation came back to Evelyn then: 'Big Brother is watching...Your phone tracks your every move.'

"Hit this button and it turns the map into a satellite image," Samantha said.

"Amazing! Are there any other apps I should have?"

"You have Google Earth, right?" Evelyn looked blank. Samantha rolled her eyes to the ceiling in exasperation. "Parents are so computer illiterate."

"I am *not*."

Samantha giggled. "You don't even know what apps you have on your phone."

Evelyn had to concede that point, but she wasn't intimidated by technology. She wondered why people assumed a housewife (for that's how they saw her, not as an artist, or even as an independent adult) would be computer illiterate. She paid the bills online, bought clothes and presents online, checked the weather, monitored their investments, mapped her walks, took photos, sent messages, followed her children on social media, video chatted, and played remote chess with her son. She may not have been entirely up-to-date, and she certainly had no interest in sharing her every movement and thought on Twitter, but she was hardly computer illiterate.

That evening Samantha installed Google Earth on the desktop computer in her father's study and showed her mother how to call up a street view of Gail's apartment in Paris.

Later Evelyn would reflect on this day and what a double-edged sword technology could be.

CHAPTER THIRTEEN

To avoid Ramon, Evelyn stayed indoors on Tuesday. She just wanted him to come, do his job, and leave. Still, she worried he might come to the French doors, either to apologize or to make certain he hadn't lost the account. She worried that Sam might overhear, and dreaded having to explain herself to her daughter. It would be too embarrassing.

She set up her easel on the far side of the living room and began sketching on a large canvas. Samantha practiced standards from the 1930s on the baby grand piano. She played "The Way You Look Tonight" three times, then "These Foolish Things."

"I've always loved that song," Evelyn said. "The images are so evocative of loss, and of the time period."

"Each verse is like a haiku," Samantha said. Then she sang two verses as she played. She had a beautiful singing voice. "I missed this when I was at school. The pianos in the music lab suck."

The front doorbell rang. Evelyn put down her pencil. "I'll get it. You keep playing." She was prepared to meet Ramon at the door. Instead, it was Connie, who held one of Evelyn's sixteen-by-twenty-inch watercolors.

"You changed the frame," Evelyn said.

"Do you like it?"

"It looks nice. Less formal."

"Take a closer look. Do you really like it?"

Evelyn examined it and nodded. "Yes, it looks good."

"It's a giclée print."

"No."

"Yes."

"Wow."

"I know, right?"

Evelyn peered more closely and shook her head. "I can't tell it from the original."

"It works best with watercolors. Oil paintings are more problematic — a giclée can't quite capture the texture of oil, but you have to be up close to notice. I was hoping to pick up some others to have them scanned. I brought the van." She had a panel truck with racks specifically built for transporting paintings. Ramon's truck was just pulling up behind it. Evelyn stepped aside to let Connie in and closed the door.

"I get a professional discount with the printing company," Connie said, "so whenever you're ready to scan something, bring it to me. It's cheaper than going direct." She seemed to notice the music then for the first time. "Who's playing?"

"My daughter."

"She's good."

"She's always enjoyed it."

Evelyn led the way to the kitchen and poured them each a glass of white wine. Ramon passed by the window with his chemical kit and a long skimming pole with a sieve attached to one end. "I see you got The Pool Boy," Connie said, salaciously licking her upper lip. "Didn't I say he was gorgeous? Has he...? Have you...?"

"What?" Evelyn asked, thinking that her recent dalliance (if she could even call it that) showed in her expression.

"You know," Connie said suggestively. "I wouldn't mind, really. He's been very good to me, but I never figured he was exclusive."

"I'm married!"

"That never stopped *me,* and I have to say — he is good. I look forward to Fridays."

Evelyn wondered if Connie was pimping for him, or just bragging. "Well, why shouldn't you? You're both young and single. Anyway, I'm old enough to be his mother."

"He's a very interesting young man. Ambitious."

And poised, and handsome, and he has wonderful hands, Evelyn thought. *And I'm still married. I shouldn't have led him on.*

They hadn't noticed the piano had gone silent, and Samantha walked in on their conversation. "Old enough to be whose mother?"

Connie made a gesture with her head and Samantha glanced out the Dutch door.

"What happened to Mario?" she asked.

"He retired," Evelyn said.

"Don't be getting any ideas," Connie teased Samantha.

"Oh please, doing the pool boy? That's such a cliché. I'm Sam, by the way."

"I think you've met before," Evelyn said.

"No, I don't think so," Connie said, proffering a hand. "I'm Connie Whitfield, or Katz — take your pick. I was married to your father's partner for a while."

"Oh," Samantha said, her lack of interest all too apparent. She looked at the wineglass in her mother's hand. "I wonder what Daddy would say about drinking in the middle of the day."

"Considering his boozie lunches, not much," Connie answered.

Evelyn looked quizzically at Connie.

"Well," Connie said, "that's what Albert used to say. You know — three martini lunches?"

Samantha looked at the small painting on the dining room table. "I remember this. Didn't you paint this when I was nine or ten?"

"It's a giclée print," Connie said. "I have the original at my gallery. You know, I represent your mother's work now."

"Since when?" Samantha asked her mother.

Connie answered instead. "We sold her first painting last November. Now she's going to go into business selling prints and gifts with her artwork on it."

"Really?"

"It's not definite," Evelyn said.

"Nonsense," Connie countered, "you'll be a big success."

"Good for you, Mom," Samantha said, pouring herself an iced tea.

The front door opened and closed and Howard came in. "You're home early," Evelyn said.

"I have to pick up some papers and rest. I have a dinner meeting tonight. What the hell is that truck and van doing in our driveway? I had to schlep my briefcase from the street."

"Mea culpa," Connie said.

Howard glowered at her, but his attention was pulled toward the backyard where Ramon was skimming blossoms from the pool. "Who the hell is that?"

"The new pool boy. Connie recommended him."

"What happened to the old one?"

"He retired."

Howard scowled. "I liked the old one." He filled a glass of water and left the room with Samantha at his heels.

"I can't believe you never met Sam before," Evelyn said.

"The only parties you ever hosted were during the holidays, and I think she stayed upstairs. Kids don't seem much entertained by drunken adults."

"I was never drunk."

"Maybe not, but the rest of us were tipsy. Is she home for the summer?"

"She leaves next week for Paris."

"Lucky her."

"It'll be fun," Evelyn said, and told Connie all about the girls' plans. "I can follow her on this app, so I know where she's at. And if I want to see what she's seeing, I can just go on Google for a satellite image or street view."

"God, I wouldn't want *my* mother knowing where I am."

"Sam doesn't care; she doesn't have anything to hide."

"You have no sense of privacy, do you." This was offered not as a question but as a statement.

"I've never done anything I was ashamed of," Evelyn answered, knowing as she said it that it was a lie. She was ashamed of murdering a poor gopher, whose only crime had been to try to survive, and she was ashamed for almost seducing the pool boy. But she wasn't about to admit that to Connie.

CHAPTER FOURTEEN

It was a large, somewhat unwieldy canvas. She didn't often do paintings of this size, but on Monday she set her biggest easel before the herb garden and began painting. That morning the gardeners arrived, two men who spoke no English but went about their tasks, blowing off the patio around the fountain, mowing grass, trimming hedges, pruning bushes, and watering. Samantha came out in a bikini and lay back on the chaise lounge with a paperback. Evelyn was so engrossed in her work, she didn't notice her daughter for almost half an hour.

"Oh, what are you doing here?"

"Do I have to have permission?"

"No, of course not. I mean, when did you come out? You surprised me."

"Awhile ago."

Evelyn noticed the book. "What are you reading?"

"*The Splendour Falls* — Susanna Kearsley. It's really good."

"Romance?"

"Not really, at least not yet. There're hints of that, but it's mostly a mystery."

The blower began blasting. Evelyn tuned it out and continued to paint. Samantha tuned it out and continued to read.

"Mom?" No response. "Mom!"

"What?"

"Company."

Evelyn looked over her shoulder and saw Ramon striding up the lawn. He was hatless and carried a folder. He smiled tentatively, nodded to Samantha, and stopped before Evelyn, hanging his head. "I wanted to talk to you," he said, glancing quickly at Samantha to judge if she was close enough to hear. "Maybe this is a bad time."

"About what?"

He looked everywhere but in her eyes. He whispered, "I wanted to apologize."

"It's not important; forget it."

They heard a splash as Samantha dove into the pool.

He looked into her eyes then with a look of such contrite gratitude that Evelyn was almost compelled to take him in her arms to comfort him. He was a sweet boy, really, she thought. He'd just been carried away, and he was now truly remorseful. She put a hand on his forearm and smiled. "Don't worry about it." He looked relieved and she felt the tension between them melt a little. "You didn't have to make a special trip."

"I didn't get a chance to talk to you last week." He seemed to see the painting for the first time. "You moved the gopher hole."

"I thought it should be a hidden element, something you don't see at first glance. A sort of subliminal message."

"I've been thinking a lot about what I could do…" He looked quickly toward the pool to see if Samantha was listening and was startled to find her holding onto the coping and looking straight at him. He smiled and winked, receiving a cold glare in return and, turning back to Evelyn, finished, *sotto voce*, "…to make it up to you. I like working for you and I thought you might be interested in a business proposition."

"I'm sorry, I don't follow."

"I brought a prospectus," he said, holding out a presentation folder.

"I don't really *do* business."

He looked confused. "But you're starting your own business. You're opening your own shop."

"That's different."

"Not so different. Here, just read this and think it over. We could be partners. I would do all the work. You would make half the money."

Do I really look so gullible? Evelyn wondered. She said, "I don't think Howard would approve."

"I wasn't talking about going into business with your husband."

"Any money we invest is money Howard earned, so he has to approve it. I'm not even sure he'll let me open my store."

"Does he monitor everything you do?"

In fact, Evelyn did have a certain degree of latitude. She paid the bills. She held joint brokerage, checking, and savings accounts with Howard. If she were secretive, she could free up $10,000 or $15,000 to make an investment. Not that she would ever waste that resource on a scheme her pool boy proposed. She might, however, use it to fund opening her own shop. Connie hadn't said how much she was willing to invest, but she'd implied she wanted to be a partner. And even if she couldn't count on Howard's consent, Evelyn was sure her father would help out.

Ramon was saying something. She looked at the prospectus in her hand. "I'll take a look at it, but don't get your hopes up," she said.

He smiled, suddenly turning on his radiant charm. "I think we would make good partners. I know I could trust you. You're honest and levelheaded."

"I won't disagree with you there," she said, though she was aware he was just trying to butter her up. He didn't know her well enough to say if she was honest *or* levelheaded.

"You're a very attractive lady."

Evelyn was amused at his clumsy attempt at manipulation. "Ramon, I'm old enough to be your mother, and we both know it."

"I only speak the truth."

"Besides, I know about you and Connie."

"Connie?"

"Connie Katz?"

He looked genuinely puzzled.

"Maybe you know her as Connie Whitfield?"

The light dawned in his eyes. "Oh, Constance. She's...a nice lady." He shrugged and looked away. "We have an arrangement. We each have our needs."

"I'm not disapproving," Evelyn said playfully, enjoying his discomfort. "You're both consenting adults, and she's not much older than you. Have you shown her your prospectus?"

"You're the first I've shown it to."

"I'll look at it," Evelyn said, with no intention of following through. She wanted to bring the conversation to a close. She wanted to get back to work. "You'll be coming tomorrow, as usual?"

"Yes, tomorrow."

When he was gone, Samantha pulled herself out of the pool and began toweling off. "Who was that guy?"

"Our pool boy, Ramon. You saw him last week."

"Did I? I didn't like the way he looked at me. He's a little creepy."

"You shouldn't judge him at first glance. He's a very nice young man."

"He's a narcissist. You can see that a mile away," Samantha scoffed. "God's gift to women."

CHAPTER FIFTEEN

The Sunday street fair encompassed four blocks of small, white marquees where vendors sold jewelry, dresses, sweaters, hats, slippers, toys, handmade furniture, art glass, pottery, soap, perfume, photographs, lithographs, puzzles and wreaths, CDs, musical instruments, steampunk paraphernalia, wooden sculptures, garden spinners, food and wine. People milled about in front of the booths and jostled past knots of gawkers and baby strollers. Bubbles were floating in the air, and a band played covers of old rock-and-roll favorites.

In the din, Evelyn could hardly hear herself think. She'd been waiting by a booth of hand-loomed blankets for fifteen minutes. Then she saw Brooke and broke into a smile of recognition.

"I wasn't sure you were going to make it," Evelyn said, "and I didn't want to move because I wasn't sure I could find you in all this mess."

"I'm sorry, I got tied up at the shop. I tried calling, but all I got was your voicemail."

Evelyn took out her phone and looked at the screen. It showed three missed calls. "It's so loud, I didn't hear it ring. I should have you on Friend Finder."

"What's that?"

"An app that lets you know where your friends are. My daughter showed me. She's going on a trip, and I'll be able to track where she is in Paris. Here, look." She touched the screen and a map appeared that showed their location and that of Samantha. "See, she's down on the wharf having lunch with her roommate. They're leaving Thursday."

"That's cool."

"It comes with your phone. You just have to activate it. Do you want to friend me?"

Brooke, who would have balked at letting her parents follow her movements, was delighted at the prospect of forming a closer bond with one of the artists she admired. She was flattered that Evelyn considered her a friend, instead of a mere business acquaintance. "Sure."

Evelyn touched the button that said Invite Friend, scrolled through her contacts, and tapped Brooke's name. Brooke's phone pinged. "Now, click Accept." Brooke did as instructed. "There, now we're connected. Then if we're separated, it'll be easy to find one another."

"That's handy. Do you want to grab something to eat, or do you want to shop? We still have almost an hour before we meet with Connie. She's found two available shops. One of them isn't even listed yet."

"I think we found the right spot for a shop," Evelyn said over lunch Monday at The Grotto. She and Samantha were sitting on the terrace overlooking the marina. "It's a flower shop now. The owner is retiring. I'm taking your grandfather to see it tomorrow. Would you like to come along?"

"I can't; I still have to pack. I thought Daddy was against it."

"He's not on board yet, but I'm working on him. I don't know what he expects me to do with myself, now that you kids are grown."

"I think it's a good idea."

"Besides, I must be one of the only women of my generation who's never held a job. Your father always made enough, and I had you kids to look after."

"Painting is a job."

"Not if you don't make money at it. You wouldn't believe how much more satisfying it is to be paid for your work. It's a kind of validation."

"Of course it would be."

"Your father doesn't understand that. He thinks I should just be content to paint as a hobby. But why shouldn't I make money at it?"

"Don't look at me; I'm totally supportive. Go for it, Mom. You deserve to do what you want."

"It's so nice to have a daughter who gets it. Maybe you can talk to your father."

Samantha held up her hands in protest. "Don't put me in the middle. I just want you to be happy."

"You can be subtle."

"Dad doesn't understand subtle," Samantha said, and immediately changed the subject. "Can I take another suitcase? I don't think I'll have room for everything."

"You don't have to take your whole wardrobe with you. Besides, you're not going on safari. You can buy whatever you need in Paris."

On Tuesday, Evelyn and her father paid a visit to the flower shop. When they were done, Bill Hightower made a call to the landlord to set up a meeting.

Evelyn listened to the one-sided conversation, grateful to have someone handling those legal aspects that were beyond her expertise. He hung up and said, "It's all set. We'll meet with him on Friday, just to feel out his position."

"Do I have to go?"

"I think it would be a good idea. It's your name that'll be on the lease, if it goes that far."

Evelyn's head was swimming with facts, figures, and possibilities as she drove up the steep drive and parked her white BMW in the middle bay of the garage. She found Samantha in her bedroom, with two large suitcases open on the bed.

"I can't fit it all in," Samantha whined. "I need another bag."

"An extra bag will cost an extra fifty dollars. Just pack what you can. I'll send the rest by FedEx. It'll be cheaper."

"Ah, perfect." Her mood seemed to lift immediately.

"Have you confirmed your reservations?"

They had decided that Samantha would fly to Los Angeles to meet up with Gail at the airport before their nonstop flight to Paris.

"Yeah. You're sure you wouldn't rather drive me to Gail's instead?"

"No, flying from here saves me three hours of driving, plus gas. And if we got caught in LA traffic, you could miss your flight."

They packed, refolded clothes, and put aside bulkier items to be shipped later.

Remembering the day of the week and the prospectus she had no intention of reading, Evelyn asked, "Did you notice if Ramon came by today?"

"He was in the backyard."

"Did he say anything?"

"He left a note. It's downstairs on the kitchen table."

The note asked if she'd like to meet to discuss the prospectus. It annoyed her. Why did he think she would be interested in going into business with him? She'd barely said two words to him, and now he was pestering her with this business proposition. She was also annoyed with herself for encouraging him. Her mother had been right. It was best to maintain a reserve with the hired help. She wished he'd just go away.

CHAPTER SIXTEEN

Wednesday night Howard took them to Bouchon for a bon voyage dinner. Thursday morning Evelyn saw Samantha off at the municipal airport. It was a quiet ride back, and the house seemed emptier when she returned. Samantha called to say she was through security. They chatted until she had to board. That evening Evelyn made beef stroganoff and sat down with a Chardonnay to wait for Howard.

He came home late, as usual. "Did Sam get off all right?"

"Their flight from LAX was delayed half an hour, but they got off okay. I've been tracking them online."

He looked tired. He made himself a martini with Hendrick's Gin, a dropper of dry vermouth, and a twist of lemon peel, and sat down at the kitchen table. "I have a meeting at Calysta Vineyards Saturday afternoon. It's in Atascadero. They always expect us to try their product, and the last thing I need is a DUI, so I think I'll stay overnight in their guesthouse."

"You could always spit like a professional taster."

"The meeting will probably spill over into dinner, and it's a two-hour drive home. It's safer to stay over."

She knew it was childish, but the thought of being alone overnight left her feeling abandoned. "Maybe I could come with you."

"It's a business meeting, Evy."

"At least we'd have time alone together on the drive."

"I'll be home Sunday afternoon," he said wearily. He sipped his martini. "By the way, I got a call from your father today. I don't appreciate being pressured to support your crazy business venture."

82

"I didn't ask him to call."

"As far as I'm concerned, if your father wants to bail you out, all the more power to him. I wash my hands of it. I've given you my advice. If you don't want to take it, fuck it."

Evelyn felt like she'd been slapped. *Sticks and stones...*But words did hurt. He swore at times, but usually he swore at inanimate objects. She assumed he was under pressure at work, and it came out in harsh words aimed at her. It was always worse if he'd been drinking. She said, "You've had too much to drink."

"I haven't even started."

She stood up without a word and left the room. She wasn't going to engage in verbal sparring. She put on a Chris Botti CD to soothe her nerves, and sat down with a book in the living room. She looked at the words, but she was too keyed up to read.

Twenty minutes later, Howard came in. His martini glass was full again, but rather than the belligerent air she was expecting, he was contrite. "I'm sorry I snapped at you," he said; "it's been a long day." The words helped mollify her mood momentarily, until he added, "But don't expect my help with this business thing. You do what you want, but I don't want anything to do with it."

She was sorry he was so resolute, but in some ways that made it easier. She might not count on his support, but neither did she have to consider his reservations. Taking on a project and making a success of it was hard enough without having to listen to naysayers. Now she would rely on Connie and her father for advice and leave Howard out of it. If she succeeded, she'd have the satisfaction of knowing she did it without him. If she failed, she'd quietly let it go and fold up shop, without listening to Howard telling her how he would have done it differently.

Friday Evelyn called Connie to see if she'd like to go out for dinner Saturday evening, but Connie was going to be visiting her sister in Los Angeles. She called Brooke, to see if Brooke would like to come to the house for dinner (she'd never been to the house), but Brooke had a date. She called her father, but he and her mother had tickets for a jazz concert. "Why don't I take you to lunch on Sunday?" her father said. "I've been meaning to try that new brewpub. You can pick up your paintings to have them scanned."

She saw Howard off just after noon that Saturday. Faced with an afternoon and evening alone, Evelyn threw herself into her work and made good progress on the new canvas. At twilight the landline rang. She let it go to voicemail. Whoever it was hung up before leaving a message. A minute passed before the phone rang again. Still no message. The third time Evelyn picked up the phone. "Hello?"

There was silence on the other end, or not quite silence — she could tell it wasn't a dead line. Then a female voice in a fake German accent said, "Ven ze cat iss avay, ze mice vill play."

A crank caller. "Who is this?" Evelyn demanded. It was a rhetorical question; she expected no answer.

But an answer came. "A friend."

There was something familiar about the voice, but she couldn't place it. Then the line went dead. She hadn't received a crank call in years. Alone in the house at night, she was suddenly frightened. Was someone watching the house? *Ven ze cat iss avay* — Howard was away. The caller knew Howard was away. What kind of sicko called with enigmatic messages in the middle of the night?

The isolation that brought her serenity by day, now left her feeling vulnerable by night. The houses on this hillside were barely visible from the street, hidden away behind trees and hedges, walls or gates. The result was total privacy, a blessing when you wanted peace, a curse when you craved the safety of close neighbors. This was the kind of place Charles Manson had chosen to invade. It didn't take much imagination to realize that a murderous gang or satanic cult could take over any one of these homes and torture or kill its occupants, and not one of the neighbors would be the wiser. *Ze mice vill play.*

She went around the house locking doors and closing windows and shades. She called Howard, but it went immediately to voicemail. She hung up without leaving a message, then called back and left a short message. A minute later, she texted him to call her. She considered calling her father, but she knew he'd insist on her coming to the beach house overnight, and the thought of walking from the front door to the dark garage at night, when a possible stalker was lurking in the shadows, made her uneasy. Besides, she didn't want to appear hysterical in her father's eyes.

Howard kept a pistol in his desk in the study, but the key to the desk was in Howard's pocket. She took the fireplace poker up to her bedroom and crawled under the covers with a book.

She dreamt she was in a room with a tall ceiling, surrounded by dark windows that reflected her own image. From the corner of her eye, she was aware of another face in a window that she dare not look at directly. It would go away if only she willed it. Then she was running, pursued down the corridors of a grand hotel, frantically searching for a closet to hide in, or a door to a crowded lobby. She felt hot breath on her neck (...*Ze mice vill play!*) and swung around to confront her pursuer.

She came wide-awake at the sound of a loud crash, her arm still vibrating. Pushing herself up on her elbows, eyes wide, she took stock of her surroundings. In the faint glow from the bathroom nightlight, she could make out the vague shapes of the bedroom furniture. Only then did she become aware of the poker still clutched tightly in her hand. She dropped it, scooted over to Howard's side of the bed, and turned on his lamp. Her heart was pounding. The illuminated clock read 3:24.

On her side lay the remains of a shattered lamp. Fully awake now, she got out of bed to clean up the mess and examine the damage in more detail. The poker had gouged the top of the nightstand. She felt lucky she'd been unable to get Howard's gun from his desk. What might she have shot in her sleep? When the lamp was in the trash, she climbed back into bed, leaned against the headboard on Howard's side, and read until fatigue overtook her shortly after five.

She awoke in the full light of day with a kink in her neck. That morning she opened all the blinds and walked around the perimeter of the house. There was no sign that anyone had been outside last night — no footprints or gum wrappers or cigarette butts. Nothing to suggest a stalker. It was just a crank call then. *Ven ze cat iss avay, ze mice vill play.* But it had rattled her, and she still felt troubled that her peace of mind could be so easily disrupted by a few silly words. "A friend," the voice had said. Some friend. She called Howard again, and again the call went straight to voicemail. That was disturbing, but there was nothing to be done about it.

She showered and ate. Then she checked Friend Finder. A map of Paris appeared on the screen. Samantha was in the Overstreets' apartment on Quai Malaquais, beside the École des Beaux-Arts, on the left bank of the Seine, across from the Louvre. Evelyn tapped the message button and the dictation icon and spoke into her phone. "Text me a few photos of the apartment." The words appeared onscreen, and she pressed Send.

She was just getting ready to meet her father for lunch, when Howard came in with his overnight bag and briefcase.

"I didn't know you would be home so soon. I'm having lunch with Daddy. Do you want to come?"

"No, I'm tired. I just want to relax."

"Why didn't you call? I left messages. I even texted."

"Is Sam okay?"

"She's fine. There was a crank caller last night. I just wanted to hear your voice."

Howard opened his briefcase, retrieved his phone, and looked puzzled. "Huh. I turned it off during the meeting. I guess I forgot to turn it back on. Yeah, here's your messages. Sorry."

"I don't know why you bother with a cell phone; I can never reach you."

"I'm on the phone all week as it is. Why would I want to be on call when I'm out of the office?"

"Well," Evelyn sighed with exasperation, "it might be nice if I could get hold of you when I need you."

Her father looked old and tired, she thought, or maybe that was just transference. In her mind he was a perpetual sixty, and she was still thirty-two. But when she looked in the mirror, or met with her father, the passage of time was all too clear. He was seventy-seven, and she would soon turn fifty. Maybe Howard was right. Maybe she shouldn't be thinking about starting a business. She certainly didn't need to make money. In fact, going into business might be a financial drain. What percentage of businesses failed in the first year? Why did she think she would fare any better? It was tempting to dismiss it as a foolish whim she had considered, but had in the end let pass.

Then over lunch, she was once again sucked into her father's enthusiasm for the venture, and she realized several things: First, she didn't want to disappoint her father. He would be supportive, no matter what her decision. But if she let the opportunity pass her by, she knew he would be disappointed. To justify his faith in her, she didn't have to succeed; she just had to try. Second, she really did get a kick out of sharing her work with the public. A painting her father had hung in an office, or given to a friend, didn't give her half the satisfaction she got from a painting that hung in The Whitfield Gallery for the public to peruse, not to mention the charge she got when a painting actually sold. Becoming a professional conferred a different status to her work. Third, and perhaps most importantly, she wanted to prove to her children (and to Sam in particular) that she was more than a mere housewife with a hobby. She wanted more than their love; she wanted their respect.

"I bubble-wrapped all of the paintings," her father was saying, as Evelyn's phone chimed. "Where are you having them digitized?"

Evelyn looked down at her phone. "It's a message from Sam," she said. "It's nine fifteen p.m. in Paris. She's sent a photo of the café where they're having dinner." She held up her phone for her father to see. "Hold on." She tapped Friend Finder, and a map of Paris showed them the location of the restaurant. "It's called Le Brasserie de la Bourse." The phone chimed again to announce another message. Evelyn read, "Out to dinner with students from the art school next to the apartment. Paris is great! Wish you were here."

"Isn't that amazing?" Bill Hightower marveled. "Half the world away and it's like she's across the street."

It seemed crazy that she could know where her daughter was, and communicate as easily as if she were in the next room, and she never knew when Howard was on his way home for dinner, or had stopped off at the gym. If she knew, she could anticipate his arrival and have a hot dinner and a drink waiting when he walked in the door.

That night, as Howard showered, she surreptitiously sent a Friend Request to his phone. The app on his phone asked, "Would you like to share your location with Evelyn Marsh?" She tapped Yes. A message pinged. It read, "Evelyn Marsh is now following you." She deleted the message. It was as simple as that. After all, what he didn't know couldn't hurt him, she thought at the time.

CHAPTER SEVENTEEN

Howard was having his mug of morning coffee in the kitchen when the cell phone in his briefcase began playing "The Buffoon."

"Crap," he said, fishing out the phone. Evelyn raised her eyebrows, asking a silent question. "Marsh here," he said cheerfully. He listened for a moment. "I don't know. Hold on a minute." He riffled a file from his briefcase and pulled out a paper. "No, not here. Hold on. Give me a minute to turn on the computer." He picked up his briefcase and headed for the study.

Evelyn cleaned up the breakfast dishes and poured the remaining hot coffee into an insulated commuter cup for Howard to take on his way to work. She checked Robert and Samantha's Facebook pages, and Friend Finder, comforted that her daughter was sightseeing in Montmartre, where the day was getting long. She texted her, "Thinking of you. Wish I were there."

A moment later a reply came back: "Wish you were here, too. It's incredible."

Evelyn texted back: "Take a picture where you are right now and text me."

A minute later she received a photo of the Basilica of the Sacré-Coeur.

"Thanks for letting me tag along," Evelyn texted back. "Love you."

"Love you, too," was the reply.

A few minutes later, Howard came back to the kitchen. He put down his briefcase and finished off his cold mug of coffee. Evelyn tried to show him Samantha's texts and photo.

"Not now," he said, "I'm late. I'm going to run to the bathroom. Then I have to get out of here."

Evelyn saw him duck down the hall toward the half bath and thought that it was ridiculous for him to feel rushed; he was a full partner. He could come and go as he pleased. No one was looking over his shoulder (as her father had done for so many, many years), but leaving at eight thirty had become ingrained in his daily schedule.

"Is there any hot coffee left?" he asked when he came back.

"I'm way ahead of you," Evelyn said, handing him the commuter cup.

"All right, I'm outa here," he said.

He rushed out, and a moment later she heard the front door slam. She had just put a kettle on the stove when she noticed Howard's briefcase on the floor. She snatched it up and sprinted for the front door.

The black BMW was just passing the front walk as she burst out of the door. She called out. Howard stood on the brakes, then backed up to the walk. Evelyn opened the passenger door and put his briefcase on the front seat. "Thanks," he said.

"Honestly, I think you'd forget your head if it wasn't screwed on tight," she said.

She watched as the car plunged down the drive, then she turned back to the house.

She'd just closed the door when she heard "The Buffoon" playing from Howard's study.

The phone stopped ringing as she entered the office. It lay on the desk beside the computer. She would have to deliver it to the office. But in light of the fact that he'd taken an earlier call at home, which was unusual, she thought he might have urgent business. It might be important to return the call quickly, and he would appreciate knowing who had called. She would call ahead to the office and give Holly the number to

90

pass on to Howard when he arrived. She pressed Recent Calls. It was, as she later reflected, the moment when everything changed. She would often think that life had been so much simpler before that damned phone rang.

At first, she was confused. She recognized Connie's number. She wondered, with a sense of foreboding, what business Connie could have with Howard. Then Howard's phone pinged to announce an incoming text message. She tapped the message icon, and a list of text messages came up. There were a number of people on the list, including herself. The latest message was from CK: "Can't make it tonight. Have a business meeting." CK — It could stand for someone else, surely. Charles Krug. Curtis King. Chester Kavanaugh. She tapped his Contacts list. Next to CK was the phone number she knew by heart.

She went back to messages and tapped the last one from CK. It opened a string of messages. It seemed he had never bothered to delete a message (perhaps he didn't know how). She scrolled through thirty or forty. They were mostly prosaic questions, the scheduling of assignations and requests to bring a bottle of wine or something from the market — the sorts of texts you might expect between a married couple. Some of these were followed by emojis — smiley faces, winking eyes, hearts. But one was a photo attachment that took her breath away: a close-up, glistening twat shot that left nothing to the imagination, and the caption, "Come and get it!"

She heard the black BMW roar up the drive. She closed the messages, put the phone back on the desk, and ran to the living room. She'd just taken up her paintbrush when the front door slammed shut. A minute later, Howard came in with his phone. He held it up in explanation. "Forgot my phone. Gotta run!" Then she heard the front door slam and he was gone.

CHAPTER EIGHTEEN

That turned Evelyn's life upside down. She spent the entire day measuring the extent of Howard's betrayal. It wasn't so very unusual. Unfaithful husbands were a dime a dozen, a tired cliché. Conniving women were a cliché. The wronged wife was a cliché. But she had thought they were better than that. She had thought that, like her parents, they would remain bonded by a lifetime of shared experiences. Without her even realizing it was happening, their marriage had become a sham, a sick joke for others to talk smugly about.

It was a shock to discover she'd been so clueless. There had been a day (When exactly? Six months? — A year since?) when Howard had violated their vows, had come home one day and looked her in the eye, and smiled at how easy it was to fool her, and life had continued on as she failed to recognize she'd been duped.

She had only to think of Ramon to remind herself that no one was immune to longing. But it was one thing to fantasize and quite another to risk everything for a few moments of passionate abandon. Thinking about it now, his lack of desire in his own bed now made sense, for having spent his passion in another's, he had none left for his wife. However, it really wasn't the physical betrayal that struck her hardest. It was in the hours he must have spent in intimate conversation with that fucking bitch, hours he could have spent in conversation at home. And what had he said about her? What had they said about her behind her back? How had he justified his lack of self-control?

That first afternoon every negative emotion boiled over. She was by turns angry, hurt, humiliated, indignant, disappointed,

92

depressed, furious, filled with spite and seething with rage. Her heart pounded until it hurt.

She left the house to walk and think, trying to step outside herself and consider how to respond rationally. She was tired of being used, tired of being underestimated. She walked the winding streets in a daze, all the way down to the beach, where she sat for two hours watching the waves roll toward shore, their susurrant rush calming her nerves.

She returned home physically and emotionally exhausted, slept three hours, and awoke sweaty and dull-witted. Then she took a long shower, during which she decided against confronting him immediately. This was something that had obviously been going on for some time, and there was nothing to be gained by letting her emotions get the better of her. It was in her best interests to confront him when and where she chose. Accusations and screaming recriminations wouldn't change what had already happened, and it wouldn't be to her benefit. Howard would simply justify his betrayal by pointing the finger at *her* — she hadn't fulfilled his needs; she was dispassionate in bed; she was no fun anymore, yada, yada, yada. Didn't the guilty always justify their misdeeds? She had no doubt even Hitler thought he was merely misunderstood.

How long had it been going on, she wondered. Had Howard and Connie been lovers (the image of them coupling made her cringe) when Connie had approached her asking to represent her work? And why, now, had Connie done her best to talk her into committing to a new business? Presumably to keep her occupied while Connie diddled her husband, or perhaps to soothe Connie's conscience, if she had one.

Evelyn shouldn't have been surprised, given Connie's background, and now she had to ask herself why she hadn't been disapproving when Connie had stolen Albert Katz away from his first wife. The sad truth was that Evelyn had never liked the first Mrs. Katz, Jean Katz. A childless public relations professional, she'd made the mistake of dissing Evelyn's parenting style at a company Christmas party. Evelyn was only too happy to see her go.

Did Connie think she was going to steal Howard away? Economically it didn't make good sense. She was collecting alimony from Albert Katz. If she were to marry Howard, the alimony payments would stop, and Howard would begin paying alimony to Evelyn — altogether a poor business proposition.

And what of Howard? Could she stay married to a philanderer, knowing she could never trust him? Did she want to? She had to admit the sad fact of the matter was that her life would probably not change much if they divorced. Yes, he would move out and she would be alone in the house. But she was already alone in the house from 8:00 a.m. to 8:00 p.m. The only real change would be no sex Sunday mornings, and as it was, that was no great loss. But she still thought it unfair that he should walk away with a younger, more vibrant woman to drool over, while she was of an age where the only men who would be interested in her were geriatric divorcés and widowers looking for a last Viagra-fueled fling before kicking the bucket (the occasional Ramon notwithstanding).

What would she do with herself, now that her children were grown and her husband no longer wanted or needed her? She had always been so swallowed up in the minutiae of day-to-day existence that she didn't have a clear vision of the future. Until today, the future had been a bright place, a hopeful place, a place where they would grow old together, enjoy watching their children progress with their own lives, and have grandchildren to dote over. Now it would be awkward. How were they supposed to celebrate holidays and birthdays? Where did the children's loyalties lie?

She was well aware she'd lived a coddled life, and was unprepared for life outside of the house. She'd often felt like a stage manager, facilitating the lives of her family, preparing them for their entrance onto the big stage, herself an unseen player in their dramas. That evening she played the dutiful wife, while plotting how to take her place on the big stage.

Howard came home early, a bit disgruntled.

"I thought this was your gym night," she said.

"I'm too tired. What's for dinner?"

"Lasagna, with ground beef, spinach, ricotta and mozzarella. It's on the table with your martini."

"You're too good to me."

For once, Evelyn agreed with him.

CHAPTER NINETEEN

Evelyn parked at a meter across from The Whitfield Gallery. She fed the meter and opened the trunk. Then she took a moment to compose herself. She took a deep breath, put on a bright, friendly, guileless face, picked up a stack of bubble-wrapped paintings, and crossed to the gallery. Brooke saw her struggling to open the front door and ran to help.

"Here, take these," Evelyn said. "I have another stack in the trunk, and two big ones in the backseat."

When the last of the paintings had been delivered, she said, "I was hoping Connie would be here. I've brought these to be scanned."

"She'll be back in a minute. She just went to the bank. Has your daughter left for Paris yet?"

"She's there now." Evelyn fished in her purse for her phone. She called up the Friend Finder app and showed Brooke where Sam was staying.

"That's so cool. I've been having such fun with it. I added my parents and my brother, and my boyfriend, and you, of course. I'm glad you consider me a friend."

At the sound of Brooke's voice pronouncing "...a friend," Evelyn was almost struck dumb by the recognition, but she managed to say, "I don't have many friends, so the ones I do have are important to me." Then she smiled and hoped it didn't look false, for now she thought she knew who her crank caller had been, and why the voice had seemed familiar when she'd said, "A friend." Brooke knew. *Ven ze cat iss avay, ze mice vill play.* Howard had been away, but it suddenly dawned on her — Howard wasn't the cat. She was the cat. Howard and Connie were the mice.

"It's so fun to keep track of your friends," Brooke said.

"Do you have some scissors? Let's cut off this bubble wrap."

Brooke kept up a nonstop patter about the gallery, about some of her favorite new pieces, and asked questions and made notes about each of the paintings they unwrapped. "I'm not talking too much, am I?" she asked apologetically.

"No, why do you ask?"

"I have a habit of talking too much. I'm a little sensitive about it, as you can imagine with such an unfortunate name."

"What's unfortunate about Brooke?"

"Brooke? Nothing. But Brooke Bass?" Brooke raised her eyebrows as if to say "Get it?" Seeing Evelyn's blank stare, she explained. "As in Big Mouth Bass? That's what they called me in grade school, until I got to high school. Then it was Big Boobs Bass. I've always hated my name."

Connie walked in and saw them cutting the bubble wrap. "Don't bother," she said. "I still have to take them to be scanned."

"These are all the ones from my parents' house," Evelyn said. "My father is still trying to get some from friends. Then there're all those at the office."

Evelyn invited Connie and Brooke out to lunch, as though she suspected nothing. Connie accepted, but told Brooke she had to man the store while they were gone. Evelyn registered Brooke's distress, and realized that Brooke was only worried for her. It was touching. Maybe she really was a friend.

Over lunch and margaritas at Chevy's, Connie asked, "You're going ahead with this then?"

"I think so. Howard's against it. He won't help at all, but I'll have you and my father to advise me, so yeah, I think I'd regret it if I didn't at least give it a shot."

"Good, and I wouldn't worry about Howard. Men don't often see the big picture. Have you ever run a business by yourself?"

"No, never. It's a little bit daunting."

"It'll be good for you, you'll see. Running a business is a challenge, but it's so satisfying. I know there'll be times when you'll curse me for getting you into it..."

I'll curse you for more than that, Evelyn thought, *and I'll thank Brooke for the idea.*

"...but in the long run, you'll thank me for it."

Maybe she really is doing this to assuage her conscience, the home-wrecking little cunt, Evelyn thought, smiling with as much sincerity as she could muster, while the picture of Connie's glistening twat danced in her head. *Come and get it!* Oh yes, Howard would come running.

She was in a surprisingly good mood. All of the negative emotions had been dispelled in favor of a cool, calculating assessment of the strength of her adversaries. She felt like a spy in enemy territory. There was something liberating about playing a part, about being an actress in your own drama. She was in no rush. She was in the intelligence-gathering phase of the operation.

They chatted over the drinks, chips, and salsa. Their entrées arrived — Evelyn had enchiladas, and Connie tacos. *If God didn't want us to eat pussy, why'd he make it look like a taco?* Midway through her second margarita, Connie excused herself to go to the "little girls' room." She took her purse with her, but she left her phone face-up beside her plate. Evelyn was almost astounded by her good luck, but she was beginning to think there was no such thing as luck. There were forces at work, and now that she'd actively assumed her part and stepped onto the big stage, the drama would play out at a predictably measured pace. She watched until Connie turned the corner, then opened her Friend Finder app and sent a Friend Request. The app on Connie's phone asked, "Would you like to share your location with Evelyn Marsh?" She tapped Yes. A message pinged on Connie's phone. It read, "Evelyn Marsh is now following you on Friend Finder." She deleted the message and placed the phone face-up beside Connie's plate. Then she tapped Connie's name in her Friend Finder app. It was working perfectly.

Connie saw the phone in Evelyn's hand. "Did you get a call?"

"No, just checking on Sam. She's having a fun time in Paris."

The conversation then meandered into the subject of travel. Connie's phone chimed. "Sorry, a client. Let me just answer this message," she said. Her thumbs tapped out the words.

It's probably Howard, Evelyn thought. *Come and get it!*

Connie put the phone down. "I've never been to Paris. I'm not really into cities. My favorite vacation was to Aruba. Albert and I stayed in the poshest resort."

Evelyn's phone chimed. She looked at the message: "Don't bother making dinner. I have to finish drafting a lease. Then I'm going to the gym. I'll be home late."

"Problem?" Connie asked.

"No, just Howard working late again."

"That man works too hard."

"Tell me about it," Evelyn said with just a hint of sarcasm. *It's such hard work getting your rocks off.* "My father kept a strict schedule, nine to five thirty. He never worked past six at the latest, and he never brought work home. I wish Howard would take the hint."

"Better a workaholic than a lazy bum, I always say."

Ramon's truck was parked by the front walk, blocking the drive to the garage. She had no wish to see him. If she'd been another sort of woman, she might have taken him to bed to spite Howard, but she didn't yet want to stoop to his level, or give him anything he could throw back in her face. Ramon and Howard and Connie were all alike in one respect: they were opportunists with no regard for the wreckage they might leave behind. No, she had to retract the thought. In Ramon's case, that was unfair. She was just as guilty for pushing the flirtation too far. But nothing had happened she had to be (too) ashamed of (yet), and she wanted to keep it that way. She backed out of the driveway and drove to the market to pick up something for dinner.

When she returned home, she found Ramon had slipped a note into the front doorjamb. "Missed you today. I hope you've had some time to look over the prospectus. I'd like to talk to you about it. I have some exciting news that may be of interest to you." Evelyn crumpled the note and threw it in the trash. Ramon was becoming tiresome. She had more important fish to fry.

At 6:00 p.m. she checked her Friend Finder. Sam was fast asleep; it was 3:00 a.m. in Paris. Brooke was just leaving the gallery. Connie and Howard were together on Davidson Street.

Evelyn considered her next moves. She thought she might benefit from a visit to a divorce attorney. She would have to look into that, but for now it could wait.

Howard came home after 8:00 p.m.

"Have a hard day?" Evelyn asked. *You despicable prick.*

"Same ol', same ol'. That's why they pay me the big bucks."

CHAPTER TWENTY

Howard's affair had been going on for months; she was sure of it. Probably not long after Sam had left for UCLA in the fall. A reconciliation was out of the question. Trust was a fragile thing, and like Humpty Dumpty it couldn't be put together again. For all she knew, he had been cheating for years. And since she would never know for sure, she couldn't trust a word he said.

But she had no intention of meekly stepping aside and allowing Connie to become the second Mrs. Marsh. They seemed to think they could walk all over her with impunity. She'd never thought of herself as a mousey pushover, so why were they treating her with such disregard? Did either one of them think about how it would affect her children? Did they think they'd never get caught? They were like willful five-year-olds who couldn't resist the cookies, acting without considering the consequences. But unlike five-year-olds, they should have known better, and she wouldn't let them get away with it. They needed to be punished. It also didn't matter how long it might take before she found a way to exact justice. It might take months. She didn't really care. She was tired of being underestimated, underappreciated, and dismissed as a minor player in her own life. She would have her revenge.

She saw Howard off to work, if anything more attentive than usual. Midmorning found her kneeling in the herb garden.

"You look beautiful on your knees," Ramon said.

She closed her eyes and took a deep breath. She really didn't want to talk to him. "You should have called ahead. You shouldn't just show up unannounced."

"I'm sorry, is this a bad time?"

"Yes, it is. I have a lot on my mind, and I don't want to hear your salesman's pitch at the moment."

It was a harsh thing to say, but it was honest. She grasped the top of a weed, loosened the soil around its roots with a trowel, and pulled it from the ground.

"I can see this is a bad time. I just wanted to know if you've read..."

"Your damned prospectus, and the answer is no. I don't have any interest in going into business with you."

Ramon was silent for long moment. Finally he said, "I'm not asking for your help. I'm offering you an opportunity. I'm just looking for some investment capital on a project that will bring both of us a steady income. Wouldn't you like a passive income? Something that generates income while you're sleeping?"

"I don't need an investment," she said sarcastically. "I have a husband who generates income. Anyway, I don't have the money."

"Oh, I think you do. You said yourself, you're going into business."

"Yes, and I need that money to get the business going," she explained, a little peeved at having to justify herself to the pool boy. *Who the hell does he think he is?*

Ramon rolled his eyes heavenward, as though frustrated by his inability to get through to this dimwitted woman. He shook his head. "Why is it you rich people always refuse to listen until you're forced to, even when it's in your own best interests? I'm bringing you an opportunity."

Evelyn stood up, trowel in hand, annoyed now. "Oh for gods' sakes, I'm not interested. Don't bother me with this anymore. Or maybe we should just terminate our relationship entirely." She could see a flash of anger in his eyes. He hesitated, deliberating. Then a small, disparaging smile twisted his lips as he made a decision.

"I could make money posting videos to certain websites."

"Good, then why don't you just do that?"

"It would take too long. The right opportunity doesn't come around every day."

"You're young; you have plenty of time to save. Or find another partner. I'm not interested."

"I have a video you should see," he said, looking down at his phone. "I could post this one." He held the phone up for her to see.

She held her forearm to her forehead to shade her eyes and peered at the screen. The sun was bright, and at first she didn't understand what she was looking at. Then she could see it was a video of Ramon on his knees beside the chaise lounge, running his hands up and down her thighs. *How?* And then she remembered the phone sticking up from the half-pocket on the outside of his blue case.

"You bastard," she exclaimed, then she laughed derisively. "Well good luck with that. I don't think that will get you many followers on YouTube."

"No, but your husband might like to see it."

"Are you trying to blackmail me?" Evelyn thought that hilarious under the circumstances. Here Howard could see how, fully clothed, she and Ramon had cavorted while talking of books and whatnot. Howard could hardly object, when he was screwing his mistress. "Go ahead, show him. The most it will get you is a broken nose, if he cares to defend '*my honor*,' which I doubt. I expect he'll be as amused as I am." Ramon didn't seem to understand the sheer incompetence of his effrontery. It was funny. She had thought him smarter than this, and nicer. And she thought it was a good thing that Ramon didn't know of Howard's infidelity for, if he did, he would surely try to blackmail Howard, and not knowing that she already knew, Howard might have paid him to keep quiet. "Now, if we're finished here, I have a garden to tend."

But Ramon didn't move. He didn't even look ruffled. Instead he slowly shook his head like a disappointed disciplinarian who, failing to impose his will on a recalcitrant child, was about to administer corporal punishment. Evelyn tensed, her gloved hand gripping the trowel tightly in case he tried to get physical.

"I didn't want to have to do this," Ramon said, shaking his head dolefully as he tapped the screen of his phone again.

He's going to show me a video of Howard and Connie, Evelyn thought. *But where's the profit in that? Or maybe he doesn't care. Maybe he's already blackmailed Howard, and now that I've refused to sweeten the pot, he's just being vindictive.*

"I already kno..." she began to say, but stopped as he held up the phone for her to see. The setting was the same — a corner of the pool, the trunk of a palm tree, her backyard. In the foreground beside the chaise lounge, Ramon stood naked, his cock fully erect, his hand buried in the blonde hair of the naked girl who knelt before him. She was.... With a jolt of horror, Evelyn recognized her own daughter. Her heart gave a tremendous thump that took her breath away. Her mouth went dry.

"I got twenty minutes more, if you want to..."

Evelyn felt white-hot rage with a surge of adrenaline. "You son of a bitch!" She flew at him, grabbing for the phone as he snatched his hand back and thrust it over his head. He was laughing like a playground bully taunting the little kid. She lashed out with the trowel in a long arc, aiming for his face. He feinted backward, out of the way of the blade. The force of her swing made her stumble closer, and she brought the trowel up again in a backhanded swipe that glanced off his chest. She was flailing now, landing an ineffective left hook to his ribs, a kick to the shins. His laughter turned to a maniacal giggle. He knocked her left hand away with right forearm, while his left arm still held the phone high, leaving his left side unprotected. Before he could jump aside again, the trowel caught him in the ribs just below the armpit. He howled with pain, and his arm snapped down like a Venus flytrap, pinning the trowel to his torso. She yanked back trying to wrench it free. Her hand pulled out of the glove instead, and she stumbled backward, losing a sandal. He threw the trowel and glove aside and thrust the phone into his front pocket, wincing in pain at his bruised side. "Ow! You cunt. That hurt!" Then she was on him again, pummeling him with both fists. He wasn't laughing anymore. She kicked with her bare foot, aiming for his balls, but missed. When she kicked again, he grabbed her foot and yanked upward, sending her hard onto her back and knocking the wind out of her. Tears welled in her eyes as she gasped for breath. Before she could recover, he was on top of her, knees pinning her arms to the ground. "Fuck!" he said, panting. "You really hurt me." He rotated his left arm like a bird with a broken wing, feeling the knot of bruised muscle under his arm.

For a long moment, she was convinced her breath would never come back. When it did, she filled her lungs greedily and began to whimper, croaking impotent threats as she tried to buck him off, but the weight differential was too great.

"Calm down," he said. "Now you listen to me. All I'm asking is for a helping hand, okay? I'm trying to be reasonable here. I need you to cosign a loan and pay the first couple of months on the mortgage, just until the cash flow exceeds the output. This is a good investment. You'll see. Have your husband read the prospectus. He might know a good deal when he sees it."

"You seduced my daughter."

"Consenting adults."

"I don't think she consented to your video!"

"People do sex tapes all the time."

"I want that phone."

Ramon looked skyward, sighed, shook his head, and leaned over like a raptor about to eat its prey. "It'll cost you, but I'm offering you an opportunity in return. You have something I need. I have something you want. I'd rather work with you, but if I have to, I'll raise the money some other way. Amateur porn sites pay good money for videos like that."

"Pig! Get off me!"

"You want everyone to see what a little slut your daughter is?"

"Give me your phone. I'll have you arrested."

"For what?"

"I'll charge you with extortion."

"Your word against mine."

"I'll tell them you're a pornographer."

"Ha! Porn isn't illegal anymore. It's big business. It's an industry. If you give me any trouble, I'll post it on the internet." Then, as though the idea had just occurred to him, he added, "Or I could send a copy to your husband. He might see things my way."

"He'd kill you." She said it, but she didn't believe it. Howard would be angry; he would make idle threats, but in the end he would pay.

"I'll give you a couple days to calm down and come to your senses. Call me. We'll have lunch and talk business."

That said, he jumped up and strode quickly down the lawn, rotating his left arm and chuckling as carefree as a lion after a feast.

CHAPTER TWENTY-ONE

In her own quiet way, she snapped then. The business with Howard had bent her. Ramon had broken a piece of her she thought inviolable. Her complacency was traded for a cold resolve to do all she could to protect her daughter. But how?

Ramon had taunted her as he never would have taunted a man. It was infuriating. If she were a man, she would have simply used her physical strength to overpower him and take the phone. But as a woman, she would always be at a disadvantage because of her diminutive size. Women had to employ other means to gain advantage. Sometimes it was the promise of sex. Sometimes it was stroking egos. Sometimes it was analyzing and planning, instead of letting emotion cloud one's judgment. She knew she wasn't physically capable of taking on the men in her life, but she believed she could outwit them. They had so little regard for her they would never see it coming.

She played the confrontation back in her mind. How might she have fared if she were a man? She imagined a larger version of herself rushing at him, knocking him off his feet, his head hitting the coping, his unconscious body sliding into the pool. But that was so much fantasy. She could never do it.

She lay back on the chaise lounge, closed her eyes, and tried to think her way out of her predicaments — the repercussions of Howard's infidelity; Ramon's threat to her daughter. *Why had Samantha been so stupid?* Even as she thought it, she knew why: Ramon had an animal magnetism coupled with suave manners. Who could resist him?

Exhausted as the adrenaline wore off, she fell asleep with murderous thoughts stealing through her dreams, and those dreams kept looping back to the pool. Nothing could be more normal than a pool boy drowning in a pool (after a blow to the head).

She awoke in a postadrenaline funk and dragged herself to Howard's study to discover the kind of site on which Ramon was threatening to post the video. She didn't consider herself naïve, but she was nonetheless dispirited by the avalanche of the banal and perverse. One site allowed viewers to vote their preference of video after video of smut, with the tally of votes listed underneath. Each video, of which there was an unending supply, claimed thousands of viewers. That her daughter might be exposed so publicly for the entertainment of concupiscent males made her sick to her stomach. She wasn't a prude, but her sexual predilections were decidedly conventional, while so much of what she dredged up online was disgusting and — *yuk-ugh!* — unhygienic. The internet had become the new Sodom and Gomorrah. The videos all seemed to follow the same formula. The women were interchangeable almost to the point of anonymity, though she couldn't help thinking they were someone's daughters. The men were even more anonymous, either viewed from behind, and thus unidentifiable, or photographed from navel to knees, with an emphasis on the phallus as piston. Evelyn was revolted, even as she found herself becoming aroused. She wanted to turn away, yet (disturbingly) felt hypnotically drawn to the action — it was boring in its repetition, but fascinating at the same time, like watching variations of the same accident, over and over. These young women inexplicably seemed to derive intense pleasure from gagging on penises, assuming improbable sexual positions, and being anointed in come. When had sex become so distasteful? Was nothing private anymore? How could she get the video away from Ramon?

Her fantasies turned from the erotic to the homicidal. Others who knew her would have never allowed it possible that her thoughts could turn in that direction. Evelyn had a reputation for being mild mannered and compassionate. Even in her own mind her biggest crime had been the murder of a gopher. What they didn't understand, and what Evelyn had only recently come to grips with herself, was that her peaceful nature derived from a World View in which the participants were all presumed innocent. She would never kill a fly for being a fly, or a spider for being a spider. Those creatures served a purpose; she just wanted them to take their business outside, instead of setting up shop in her home, and she dealt with them accordingly. Mosquitos, however, carried disease, and were summarily executed, for while they were only being mosquitos, they presented a danger to herself and her family. Admittedly, she'd led a sheltered life. Had she ever been subjected to the backstabbing that went on in the workplace, she would never have been so innocent. However, now, in the space of a few days, she'd discovered two men and a woman who contrived to destroy her peace of mind. They threatened the life that she'd so carefully built by doing the right thing day after day, year after year, decade after decade. So this uncharacteristic turn of mind was only as unusual as the circumstances dictated.

She thought how sweet it would be, to solve all of her problems with a simple coup de grâce. She imagined running a bath for Howard, soaping his shoulders, and dropping an electric appliance (a laptop, perhaps) into the water. A quick and not-too-painful death. Then she saw the circuit breaker trip and Howard, seething with rage, drowning her in the same tub.

She thought of the murder mysteries where the heroine/murderess poisons the victim. Ramon might accept a strychnine-laced iced tea, but what then? The problem with that scenario was that she would have to dispose of the body elsewhere, and she simply wasn't strong enough to drag 170 pounds of deadweight to her car.

The fact was that the perfect murder had yet to be invented. She knew these musings for what they were: revenge fantasies. The problem with such fantasies was that in the real world people were punished for their crimes. She'd surely be caught and go to prison. And if the police found the phone before she could erase the video, they would have their motive. Then it might be surmised that the murder had been premeditated, a crime that carried the death penalty. She could probably lure him into her bed first, then claim she'd been raped. But how would she convey a sign of struggle? What then? If she were convicted of murder, at the very least she'd rot in prison, while Howard, relieved to be rid of her, would continue living in her house. Connie or some other bimbo might even step into her place, sleep in her bed, eat in her kitchen, drive her car, while she languished in a small, cold cell. Where was the justice in that? What had she ever done to deserve such ruin?

No, if she were to act, instead of standing passively by while others ruined her life, she would have to be smart and cunning. The first thing she determined was that her problem with Howard could wait. The problem with Ramon was more pressing and required her immediate attention.

CHAPTER TWENTY-TWO

Ramon's business card gave his name and telephone number, but not his address. Nonetheless, it took only a few keystrokes on the computer to find where he lived. At 8:27 a.m. Evelyn drove slowly down the row of vehicles parked behind the former apartment complex on Richland Drive that had been turned into condominiums. The Pool Boy truck was parked in its designated space. She exited the lot on Broadmoor and pulled to the curb in the shade of a pepper tree to wait. She made a move in her chess game with Robert, noted the time in Paris (5:35 p.m.), and checked Friend Finder to see where Samantha was (the Luxembourg Gardens).

In the rearview mirror she saw Ramon's truck pull out of the alley at 8:39 a.m. She watched him until he turned left at the light on State Street. Number seven was a corner, ground floor apartment with front windows on Richland and side windows on Broadmoor. She went to the door, made a pretense of knocking, and tried the knob. It was locked. Between the sidewalk and the front windows was a lush garden of agapanthus and small palms. She waded through the vegetation and peered in the front window. There was nothing to see but a Star Wars poster hung over an Ikea couch; an overstuffed chair; a coffee table; a half-empty bookcase; and a floor lamp. She went back to the sidewalk and turned the corner. At the side of the building, she stepped gingerly through a bed of ivy and paused at another window. It was hard to be discreet under such circumstances. Anyone driving down Broadmoor would see her snooping, but she was a woman dressed in an expensive, white workout outfit and didn't fit the profile of a burglar. At worst, they'd think she was looking in the window to see if a

111

friend was home. The space between the partially drawn curtain revealed the corner of a bed, a bathroom beyond, a small writing desk beneath a square, gilt-framed mirror, and a desktop computer. But for a turquoise bedspread and a cheesy post-Impressionist knockoff on the wall, it was a drab and cheerless room. The cheap furnishings gave testament of a hand-to-mouth existence. For all his plans, his business didn't seem to afford him any luxuries. Then again, perhaps he was being frugal and banking his profits. It was impossible to know which.

She continued to the alleyway at the back of the condo, nonchalantly surveying the mostly empty parking spaces, and noting that the windows on this side of the building were all small, frosted, bathroom windows, providing total privacy. She casually tried the green door at the back of number seven. The knob turned and she felt a momentary surge of excitement, until she pulled. The door didn't budge. It seemed to be bolted on the inside.

She returned to her car, feeling stymied and frustrated. Why had she even come? What had she hoped to accomplish? It had been a fool's errand — he undoubtedly had his phone with him. When wouldn't he? *If* there had been access, and *if* he'd been in the shower, she might have snatched the phone and run, but what were the odds of that ever happening?

Back in the car, she plugged her phone into its charger. Then it dawned on her — she often left her phone charging in her car. She would have to follow Ramon and see if he did the same.

CHAPTER TWENTY-THREE

She'd always found painting therapeutic. It allowed her to clear her mind of all but the patterns and colors, and the ideas that never seemed to desert her. She spent that afternoon working on her garden tableau, even as ideas for the next one floated through her consciousness. It would be an enigmatic study of a suitcase on a bed, though she was unsure if the owner of the suitcase was packing or unpacking, a man or a woman, at home or at large, at leisure or in haste, traveling for business, or for pleasure, or of necessity. Those answers would fall into place in the next few days. At the same time, while she painted, her subconscious worked on the problem of how to get the video from Ramon, or persuade him to erase it.

The next morning she was back on Broadmoor, as The Pool Boy truck began making the morning rounds. She followed at a discreet distance. Over the course of two hours, she followed him to three residences. At each stop, while he worked on the pool in the backyard, she checked his truck's cab for a charging phone, and each time she came up empty. When he pulled into a Taco Bell for lunch, she drove past without stopping, worried and disconsolate and unsure how to proceed.

He telephoned at noon the following day. "Have you talked to your husband about my proposition?"

"He doesn't need to know."

"You don't have to tell him about the video. Just show him the prospectus."

"He's not even in favor of me starting my own business. He won't support an investment scheme."

Ramon was silent a long time. She could hear road noises. She assumed he was driving. "Are we going to be business partners?"

"I can give you some money, but only if you let me delete the video from your phone. Then we can discuss business." It was a cat and mouse game. She hoped she was still the cat.

"Have you read the prospectus?"

"Yes," she lied. She couldn't quite believe he could still talk to her about business, as though he wasn't trying to extort money and threatening to publicly expose her daughter. Did he think this was a friendly game?

"You know you hurt me the other day," he said.

What was she supposed to say? Should she humor him? Apologize? "You had it coming," she said.

"It still hurts."

Good, she thought. "That's what comes of taking pictures without permission."

"I'll see you tomorrow, Evelyn, and we can discuss this like reasonable human beings."

Through the peephole, she could see him bouncing on his toes like a nervous teenager on prom night. She'd been keyed up all morning in anticipation of this meeting. She'd had two glasses of wine to calm her nerves. She was on dangerous ground.

She opened the door, ushered him, and led him to the kitchen. She was more comfortable in the kitchen.

"It's good to see you. Really, Evelyn."

There's an old expression to describe his sort, she thought — *Snake in the grass. He must have a screw loose to think I'd trust him.* "Are you going to give me the phone?"

"What are you going to give me in return?"

"I can give you three thousand dollars," she said. It wasn't exactly true. It was as much as she felt she could spare, and still have enough left over to fund her business start-up costs, for though her relationship with Connie was nearing an end, she was determined to go through with the business plan. She'd just have to find some other gallery to represent her original work, or sell it out of her own store. The idea came from Brooke, and it was a good idea.

"Three thousand isn't nearly enough. I told you what I need."

"Take three thousand and let me erase that video. Then we can discuss it."

"Evelyn, Evelyn," he said, holding his hands out in a supplicatory gesture.

She crossed her arms, and before she could step back, he enfolded her in his arms, burying his face in her hair. She tensed, feeling like a mouse in the embrace of a cat. His hands slid down to the small of her back, and his fingers began kneading her tense muscles. "Come on, don't you think we would make good partners?"

"I thought Constance was your partner."

"She's Fridays. But if you and I were partners…"

"I'm married."

"What's that got to do with anything?"

Apparently nothing, she thought, *at least in Howard's estimation. Vows were made to be broken.* "I'm old enough…" she began to say.

"…to know better?" he interrupted, diplomatically finishing the sentence for her. "Old enough to appreciate how rare it is to find someone you feel a connection with?"

"Will you take the three thousand?"

"I like it when you're not swinging at me."

"You deserved it." She hated him for thinking he could manipulate her, and for the way her body responded to his touch. Jesus, what was it about this boy? How could she command the moral high ground when her body betrayed her intentions? Was she as low as Howard?

"I'll take your three thousand, and I'll take you to bed. Then you can have the phone, and we can get down to business."

She told herself she would just have to bear it and give him nothing in return. She would be a passive vessel. She was doing it for Sam's sake. She might have succeeded in believing it if Ramon had, like Howard, been a "slam-bam-thank-you-ma'am" sort of lover. But in the time it usually took to bring Howard to orgasm, Ramon was just getting started, and he was really very good. She hated him then. She hated him intensely. She hated him hard. And it was good.

When he was spent and satiated, he said, "You can never really trust anyone until you go to bed with them."

"I hope you don't do much business with men then."

He laughed. "You know, I don't. I don't trust men much."

"That makes two of us. Give me your phone."

He rolled over, reached to the floor, and retrieved his pants. He fished in his pockets, found the phone, and passed it to her. She tapped on the photos icon, tapped the offending video, and deleted it. Then she rolled onto her back with a sense of relief, and thinking that she was in bed with a lithe young man and could spend all day getting even with Howard, she reached over and ran her hand over his hard, flat stomach. He chuckled with self-satisfaction and locked his fingers behind his head.

"You're so young," she said.

"You're so lovely."

"You're terribly cocky."

He rolled toward her and kissed her softly on the cheek. "I'm no saint, but I think we'll make a good partnership."

"Don't you feel guilty?"

"For what?"

"For taking advantage of my daughter. For blackmailing me."

"You have to use what leverage you can to get ahead in life. It's just business."

"That doesn't make it okay."

"It's not like I'm not giving you something in return. I think I'm being generous."

"You're forcing me to take risks I don't want to take."

"I'd say we both have an agenda."

She lay there thinking about it for a minute. "I don't have an agenda."

"Of course you do. You want me. You know you do."

She felt a sudden flare of rage. Sam had been right; he was a narcissist. "You're out of your mind. And I'm not going into business with you. You were wrong to take those pictures. You were wrong to seduce my daughter."

"Seduce your...? No, no, no. I think it was the other way around. She's a man-eater. Like mother, like daughter."

"Fuck you," she said angrily.

"You have, thank you."

"Fuck you, again."

"Don't be tedious."

"I'd never go into business with you."

Ramon slid out of bed and began dressing. "You'll go into business with me," he said a little sullenly.

"Why should I?"

"You didn't think I'd give you the only copy, did you?"

"What?"

"You'll cosign the loan and pay until I say."

"What are you talking about?"

"Don't be dense. You and I are partners now. I'll call the Realtors tomorrow. We can start moving on this right away. We'll need to put in an offer. This is a sweet deal. It's not everyday you find oceanfront property. This could be a gold mine."

CHAPTER TWENTY-FOUR

She eased her conscience by telling herself that it was Howard's fault. *What's good for the goose is good for the gander, or the other way around.* She wouldn't have gone to bed with Ramon if Howard had been faithful. There was even some degree of truth in that. But she also knew she had wanted to. It was complex: part revenge, part desire, part thrill at breaking the rules, part last fling before age took its toll. Partly she had done it because she knew it had been to her advantage. She'd let him believe he was in charge. She was small. She was easily led. She was vulnerable. And if he didn't know she was also dangerous, all the better. It would be easier if he underestimated her.

As she painted, dark thoughts of Ramon and Howard kept rising like koi to feed on her fears. Men. If not for her father, a stalwart, honorable man in all respects, she would have no respect for the sex. Admittedly the sampling was small. She didn't have many friends of either sex. It was an occupational hazard all artists suffered, she felt. Art was a solitary pursuit. Though she wasn't one of those artists who sacrificed her life for art. Quite to the contrary, she had sacrificed her art for a life. Her priority had always been her family. Art took a secondary role, and that, no doubt, was why the little success she had achieved was coming late in life. Which made it all the more unfair that just as she was beginning to attract the least bit of recognition, men were running roughshod over her dreams, interested only in satisfying their own needs. Her life was infested with imperfect men, like worms in a ripe apple. Why should she suffer for their duplicity?

Worse yet, why should Sam suffer? Ramon had the power to hurt Sam — if not now, then at some indeterminate time in the future. What if she were to become engaged and Ramon threatened to show the video to her fiancé? What if she were to be offered a job or promotion? What might he demand then? As long as he had that video, he could set the terms. Evelyn couldn't let that happen. She would have to erase that threat. At the very moment this idea occurred to her, a plan began to form in the darkest recesses of her mind. She would have to find a way to check the wicked before they could do more harm. Ramon had been very stupid. If he had not reminded her that unlimited copies were possible in the Digital Age, she would not have had to go to such extremes.

The first order of business was to find and destroy as many copies of the video as she could. Of course, she didn't know if there were two, or ten, or a hundred. There really was no way of knowing. That was the sad thing. It was the thing that would drive the rest of her actions. She could never be sure there weren't more copies concealed in an innocuous folder on a hard drive, lurking on a server, or hiding on a thumb drive in a drawer or safe-deposit box. Ramon, who might have multiple copies, also knew how to use them to achieve his ends, and he'd already proven himself to be unscrupulous. Anyone else who came into possession of his homemade porn might dismiss it as prurient self-indulgence and, not knowing whom it concerned, nor the power it possessed, simply disregard it as useless smut. Ramon, on the other hand, would have to go.

CHAPTER TWENTY-FIVE

Human beings are fragile things. It doesn't take much. A gun, some poison, a hammer to the head, an ice pick to the heart. It isn't difficult, if you set your mind to it, but who in their right mind can put their mind to it? Murder is abhorrent. People naturally shy away from murder, either through a sense of empathy, morality, or fear of divine or secular retribution. Society frowns on it, until politicians lead us, like pigs to the slaughter, into the next war. Then newly minted murderers are branded heroes. Was Evelyn any less heroic for risking everything to save what she loved most?

Evelyn was tenderhearted and, as everyone would attest, wouldn't hurt a fly. If God is an insect, Evelyn could expect to be welcomed into heaven with a parade. Everyone who knew her would have told you she was incapable of harming another creature, no matter how lowly. What no one seemed to realize, or acknowledge, was that she was also pragmatic. She did what she had to do, always. Ramon had awakened the snake in her by the threat he posed to her daughter. Anyone who doesn't understand that simple fact doesn't have children. A mother's first duty is to protect her children, no matter the cost. She would willingly sacrifice herself.

There were only two things that gave her pause. First, she did not want that video to be seen by anyone. Not even if only twelve jurors. Let them speculate as to motive. Let them think there was an argument and things got out of hand. It wouldn't be hard to lure him back to her bed, kill him, and claim she'd been raped. But if investigators found the video and put two and two together, they'd have a motive that could lead to a first-degree murder charge. The solution? — She would have to find and destroy the copies before she took care of Ramon. The second thing that gave her pause was the injustice of being sent to prison, while her cheating husband continued to live in her house and share her bed with his bimbos. The injustice of it rankled. So she determined she would have to do her best to get away with it. Somehow she would have to make it look like an accident, a random act of violence, or self-defense. And, of course, any planning she did would have to be untraceable.

Evelyn did her best thinking when she was sketching or painting. Art was a sort of meditation. Her mixed-media painting of the herb garden was of medium size, three feet by two feet, horizontal. The paper had a slight pebbled texture and was clipped flat to a board that she set on the easel in front of the jacaranda. She had finished the watercolor portion and was adding the final touches in pastel. The hose snaked in from the middle left. The shovel stood upright, blade half-buried, shaft topped with a sun hat. To the right of the shovel, on either side of a basil plant, were a trowel and a pair of gardening gloves. Today she added a footprint in the dirt, a shadow from the shovel, and a portrait of Bella (her late, beloved Shih Tzu) sitting by the left corner looking attentively off frame. Her paintings never contained humans, but they sometimes included animals, mostly birds, which, if she had ever thought about it, represented freedom. The only other dog had been a Golden Retriever leaping for a frisbee, that she'd sketched from a photo.

As she worked, she tried to think as a detective might think. How might she cover her tracks? She would have to learn something of forensics, which would require research. She knew enough about computers to know that the sites she visited online would be listed in the computer's history, in which case any subsequent homicide investigation would surely conclude that the murder had been premeditated. She would have to be careful. Their only home computer was in Howard's study. At first she thought of donning latex gloves to keep her fingerprints from the keyboard. That would throw suspicion onto Howard and imply premeditation on his part. However, as furious as she was with him, for her children's sake she didn't want to send their father to the gas chamber (or was it lethal injection these days?). In either case, if it were found that someone had been browsing forensic sites on his computer, Howard would know who had done the browsing, for there were only two people with access to that computer.

She knew she could browse the internet in Private Mode, which theoretically allowed her to roam the internet with impunity, leaving no record of her movements. But was that really true? Data recovery experts could retrieve deleted files, as well as information from computers burned in fires and damaged by water. How hard could it be to recover data from a fully functional machine?

At the library, hoping to do her research anonymously, she was instantly aware of security cameras as soon as she stepped through the door. She turned and left without pausing. She walked around the block, stopped in a store to buy a wide-brimmed hat, tucked her hair under the hat, and returned to the library. She strode in past the checkout desk and walked casually toward a dozen cubicles built against the far wall, each with its own computer on a small shelf. The security cameras, placed to discourage thievery, focused on the rows of bookshelves and the checkout desk. She sauntered over to a cubicle and sat down. If any camera's field of vision was wide enough to include her, it would only capture a view of her back. She went online, switched to Private Mode just to be cautious, and spent two hours searching the internet for answers to her forensic questions.

For instance, she wondered if a coroner could tell how long a body had been dead. The answer could be found online. Each time she thought of a plausible way to kill Ramon and dispose of his body, she had to ask herself how it might go wrong. How might she be tripped up? How might she be caught? Could she make it look like an accident? It would be easy enough to go to his condo, knock, and put two bullets into his heart as he opened the door. But as Ramon had remarked (and she knew from watching TV) police and business surveillance cameras could probably track the time of her passage through a particular intersection, or past a certain store. Assuming she could lure him to a place where she could strike without being observed, she would still have to be able to prove that she was elsewhere when the crime was committed. She would need an alibi. The problem, as she found from her internet search, was that science could pinpoint the time of death fairly accurately by the temperature of the body, although there was a fudge factor, a degree of error of plus-or-minus forty minutes at best. Accuracy was further degraded in the case of drowning. The more time a body spent in water (a pool, for instance), the more difficult it became to ascertain the time of death. However, even then, the time could be extrapolated from the body temperature in relation to the water temperature.

She went over it again and again in her head and kept coming up with ways the police could catch her out. One could never be too careful. Better if the time were exact. A watch broken at the scene of an accident was an excellent way to pinpoint the time of death. With an analogue watch, you could turn the hands to any time you wanted. But most watches these days were digital, the time set automatically, and watches were sturdy. Did Ramon wear a watch? Being a pool boy, she thought he probably wore a waterproof watch. It would keep ticking even when submerged. Howard had several old analogue watches that might work. She imagined having to remove Ramon's watch postmortem, and substitute it with one of Howard's. She didn't know if she was capable of doing that. And what if he fell in the water? Did bodies float? There was another question to answer. The simple act of switching watches might be hard to accomplish if the body had sunk to the bottom. She imagined having to dive into the deep end, holding her breath as she struggled to detach the watch. She saw him open his eyes and grab her wrist. The thought horrified her in a way that all this dry planning did not.

It made sense that immersion in water would confuse the time of death, but she didn't think she could drag the body far, so she would have to kill him beside the pool. If she shot him and he fell into the pool, she would have to dive through bloody water to switch watches, and that could leave traces — in her hair, on her body. Only then did another complication occur to her: Ramon and Howard might wear different-size watchbands.

Waiting for sleep to come that night, she remembered another timepiece that Ramon carried in his pocket – a phone. A cell phone would undoubtedly stop in water, wouldn't it? Could a forensics team determine the exact time? She thought they might.

Back at the library the next day, she discovered the enormous number of secrets that police could glean from a cell phone. Every day she willingly surrendered her privacy in exchange for information, without giving it a second thought. There were any number of apps requiring location services be turned on; Friend Finder and GPS directions were only the most obvious. To make information relevant to the user, searching for anything from movie theaters to restaurants, plumbers to electricians, local tides to the weather forecast, all required that location services be turned on. Even if you turned location services off, some information was stored on phone company servers, so even destroying a phone could not guarantee your anonymity. On the other hand, phone company records were not particularly accurate, only recording which cell tower your phone had connected to, and only then at fifteen-minute intervals. The only way to be sure your phone couldn't be used to trace your movements was to turn it off. One could never be too careful.

CHAPTER TWENTY-SIX

Monday was one of those beautiful mornings when the knoll was bathed in sun while fog laid in against the coast below like milk against the side of a bowl. She opened the browser on her phone and scanned the headlines. *The world is so full of such horrible things,* she thought, and the very wording of her thought brought to mind a quote of opposing viewpoint by Robert Louis Stevenson: "The world is so full of such wonderful things, I'm sure we should all be as happy as kings."

Why shouldn't she be happy? She had *a life to die for,* as Connie had said. But if she had a life to die for, she might die trying to salvage what was left of it.

She checked on Samantha, who was currently on Île Saint-Louis in the middle of the Seine. Evelyn texted: "What are you up to?" Waiting for an answer, she checked on her chess game with Robert and made a move. Her message app pinged. Sam had texted a photo of a gargoyle with the caption: "Climbed to the top of Notre-Dame this afternoon."

Evelyn heard the hiss of water in the pipes, signaling that Howard was awake and taking a shower. She went upstairs, took his keys from the top of his dresser, and hurried down to the office. She opened the locked drawer, reached for the pistol, and stopped. The only prints on the gun were Howard's, which would suit her just fine. She didn't want to add her own. She pulled a tissue from the box on the desk, wrapped it around the pistol, withdrew it, and closed the drawer, leaving it unlocked in case she had to replace the gun in a hurry. Then she ran back upstairs, put the keys on the dresser and the gun in her nightstand. Her heart was beating faster, whether from rushing or from fear of discovery, she didn't know. She dropped her robe on the bed and joined Howard in the shower. He seemed glad to have company.

"You can do my back," he said, handing her a bar of soap.

She felt vaguely repulsed by his body, as though Connie had permanently defiled it, stolen it with her touch, and no matter how much soap she used she could never own that body as she had owned it in her youth. He turned, letting the water rinse the soap off his back. She gave him the bar, expecting reciprocation. He soaped his underarms. Only after she raised her arms and cleared her throat did he seem to notice. He gave her a perfunctory lathering, then stepped around her to let the water through, grabbed a towel, and stepped out of the shower.

She couldn't help saying what was on her mind. "Where did your passion go?"

He toweled his hair. "I don't have time for passion; it's a workday."

Howard left for work at eight thirty, as he did every morning. His return home was never as predictable, except on Tuesdays and Thursdays when, for the past few months, he'd made a habit of "stopping by the gym" after work. *Connie must be a demanding trainer*, Evelyn thought bitterly, *because he always comes home exhausted.*

At ten thirty she checked Friend Finder. Howard was at the office, Connie was still at home, and Brooke was at the gallery. She called Brooke's cell phone.

"Hi, Evelyn, what's up?"

"What's your schedule look like this week?"

"I work from ten to six."

"And Connie?"

"She doesn't really have a schedule. She comes and goes. She's usually here to keep the shop open when I'm at lunch, and she never stays later than five. Why?"

"I have a new painting for the gallery. I was wondering if you might like to come by and pick it up on Thursday after work. Then we could go out to dinner, just you and me, my treat."

"I'd love to. What's the new painting?"

Evelyn described it to her. "We can go over framing options, and I'd like to get your opinion on a few ideas I have for the shop."

"Super — sounds like a plan."

"So you'll be here around when?"

"Six thirty at the latest. It shouldn't take me more than twenty minutes. I looked you up on Friend Finder. You're not too far away."

Evelyn hung up and took a minute to compose herself. She felt like an event planner, trying hard to keep all the different pieces in motion and in sync. A minute later, she called Ramon. He answered on the first ring.

"Evelyn, what can I do for you?"

Commit suicide, she thought. She said, "I don't want you coming to clean the pool tomorrow."

"Now don't be..."

"I want you to come Thursday. I'm still working on how to get Howard on board."

"He doesn't have to know."

"You know I can't. I'd rather not go behind his back. It would be easier if he approved."

"And if he doesn't?"

"Let's cross that bridge when we come to it."

"Let's not," Ramon said with an audible sigh. "Let's discuss this now. You can still come up with the money; I know you can. You have investments."

"Yes," she agreed tentatively. She could see where he was going with this.

"People in your income bracket always have investments. You have stock you can liquidate."

"Yes, but Howard might not be so easy to persuade."

"What he doesn't know can't hurt him."

Oh, but it can, and it will, Evelyn thought. "He already knows. I showed him the prospectus and told him I wanted to make an investment," she lied.

"And?"

"He wants to talk to our accountant. But I'll tell you right now, I'm not giving you any money until I'm sure you've given me all the copies of that filthy video. I want to see you delete them all." She said it, even as she knew there was no way she could possibly be sure how many copies there were. Feigning naïveté about the digital state of the world played into her hands. "Bring every copy, and bring your laptop, too. I want you here at five forty-five. You'll destroy the copies in my presence. Then you can clean the pool until Howard comes home sometime after six."

"I knew you'd see reason."

CHAPTER TWENTY-SEVEN

Given an onerous task, Evelyn would usually opt to get it over with quickly, rather than putting it off. This time she chose to put the unpleasant business off in order to capture, perhaps for the last time, two normal days. She wanted to appreciate each moment, knowing that these might be the last normal, peaceful, free days of her life. She had lived a privileged life, given every advantage by her parents and her husband. Her life had been rich with children and art and the freedom to do as she pleased, when she pleased. She had never taken it for granted. She had always appreciated her status. She wanted to remember it in every detail.

She made Howard breakfast and saw him off to work, as though he were the perfect husband, hard-working (that was true), loyal (that was not), and loving (could a man be loving and duplicitous at the same time?). She took a cup of coffee and her sketchpad to the wrought iron table by the fountain, and made preliminary pencil sketches of her suitcase painting. For a while she was able to lose herself in her work, but in the end, she couldn't help wondering if she might never hold a brush again. Was there access to art materials in prison? Were prisoners allowed to paint?

At eleven she called her father and invited him to lunch. "And Mom, too," she added.

"She'd like that. You two don't spend enough time together."

They met at the foot of Stearns Wharf and walked out the pier to The Harbor Restaurant.

"They should post warning signs," Marjorie Hightower said. "The boards are uneven. Someone is going to sprain an ankle."

"It's nothing a two-year-old can't handle," Evelyn said.

"You laugh, but just think of the liability."

They ate at a table by the window. Evelyn indulged in a cup of clam chowder, swordfish, and a glass of Chardonnay. Her mother had shrimp salad, and her father a Caesar salad.

"You seem anxious," he said.

"Do I? I guess I am." If her emotions were so apparent, how was she supposed to feign innocence?

"You want to tell us about it?"

"Oh, it's nothing." She couldn't very well say, *My husband is having an affair; I slept with the pool boy, who's blackmailing me with a pornographic film of my daughter; and I'm planning on murdering him. Other than that, everything's fine, Dad.* "It's just this business thing."

"Is Howard giving you a hard time about it?" her father asked.

"Maybe he just doesn't want you to be disappointed," her mother said.

"It's complicated," Evelyn said. "There's a lot to consider."

"Do you want me to talk with him again?" her father asked.

"No, he's not happy you called him the first time."

"You shouldn't interfere, dear," Marjorie told her husband. "It's between the kids. They have to work things out themselves."

Evelyn took a healthy swig of wine and watched a large, male sea lion come up for air.

"I finished a new painting. It's a watercolor and pastel."

"I like your oils best," her mother said.

Their plates came and they ate, making small talk about the food, and Evelyn drank her wine and watched the sea lion as it dove and came up for air and dove again. The wine eased the tension. By the bottom of the first glass, she was feeling content, and savoring each sip. There would be no wine in prison.

"I went by the gallery the other day," Bill Hightower said. "Your work holds up well next to the others on the wall. A bit pricey, but...it looks good."

"I'm glad we're digitizing everything. It'll be good to give the kids the scans. I'm sure they never saw some of those pieces, or don't remember."

Then she took out her phone and showed her mother where Sam was in Paris (her apartment on Quai Malaquais). She tapped the message button and dictated a message: "Out to lunch with Mom and Dad. Send us a photo."

A minute later, a message came back with a photo of Samantha standing by a tall window overlooking the Seine. She wondered if they allowed cell phones in prison and guessed not.

Afterwards they strolled back down the pier, smelling the brine and cooked fish smells. "It's good to be alive," she said.

"It's better than the alternative," her father said.

"Not necessarily," her mother said.

That evening she opened Friend Finder, and found Howard at Connie's as expected. She clicked "Notify Me When Howard Leaves Current Location." When he came through the door, she had a roast chicken and martini waiting at the dining room table. Later, she sat with him in the living room as he drank his second martini in front of the evening news. They talked companionably, reminding her of earlier times, and she thought she could almost forgive him his infidelities. Almost, but not quite.

The next morning she once again awoke with the intention of living one last normal day, but it was impossible. She soon regretted putting off the inevitable, because thoughts of what she was planning kept looping through her mind, along with all the ways it could go wrong. It was one thing to plan it. It was another to see it through. She wasn't at all sure she could see it through. How could it be otherwise? After all, she wasn't a sociopath.

CHAPTER TWENTY-EIGHT

After Howard had left for work Thursday morning, Evelyn took the small pistol out to the backyard. She'd never fired it and wasn't exactly sure how it worked, but she didn't think it could be too difficult. It looked like a toy. The day was calm and clear with hardly a cloud in the sky. The grass was still wet with dew and the air still cool, but she could tell from the stillness of the day that it would be a warm afternoon. She walked to the far end of the pool and turned around, surveying the property. To the south and west, she looked into the tops of native scrub oak and madrone, above which rose the occasional imported blue spruce, pine, eucalyptus and royal palm. Through the trees she could see the roof of the house directly across from the bottom of her driveway. Sharing the knoll on the north, her nearest neighbor was hidden behind a dense privet hedge.

She examined the little Ruger. She pushed the button on the bottom of the handle and the magazine popped out. It held six bullets. She pushed it back in. Then she turned to the nearest palm, its grey trunk like the leg of an elephant, pointed the gun, and gently pulled the trigger. She pulled harder. It wouldn't budge. She let out a deep sigh of relief, glad that she'd thought to test it first. What might have happened if she'd pointed it at Ramon and been unable to fire it? She saw a safety lever by the trigger guard and pushed it up. Then she raised the barrel and pulled the trigger again. This time a loud crack reverberated in her ears, splinters flew and a small hole appeared in the smooth grey trunk of the palm. She was shocked at how loud the gun was. Not that it mattered. If anyone had heard, no one was interested enough to investigate.

Midafternoon she sat in the kitchen with a cup of tea and went over her list. The first thing on the list was "test gun." She crossed that off. One part of her knew that she was only going through the motions, that she would never actually do what she planned to do. It was too far beyond the pale. It wasn't who she was. Then she thought of her daughter, and a future where the threat of exposure was always there in the background, like a hammer raised overhead, to threaten and coerce. She got up to address the items on her list.

She placed an easel in the living room in front of the French doors, and set her finished painting of the herb garden on it. She propped the French doors open. She looked out past the fountain and across the lawn to the pool. From this angle, she couldn't see the bottom of the pool. She crossed those items off the list.

Next, she texted Howard to ask if she should make dinner for him, knowing full well that this was Thursday and he would likely pay a visit to Connie before coming home.

Upstairs, she pulled on cutoff jeans over a bikini bottom, and a linen halter top over a bikini top. From the bottom of her closet, she brought out a woven grass beach basket with a cloth interior and rope handles. She made sure the safety was off before placing the Ruger in the bottom of the basket and covering it with a folded beach towel. She added a pair of latex gloves (to keep gunshot residue from her hands), flip-flops, a plastic bottle of sunscreen, and a pair of sunglasses.

Her phone pinged with a predictable text message from Howard: "Going to the gym after work. I'll grab a sandwich. Don't worry about me for dinner."

She crossed those items off the list.

She texted Brooke: "Are we still on for this evening? Six thirtyish?"

A return message arrived a few seconds later: "Looking forward to it." She crossed that off the list.

On the bed she laid a towel; panties; bra; short-sleeved T-style dress, and sandals. She transferred her essential items from a large purse to a small purse.

In the study, she took a blank sheet of paper and printed with a permanent marker: "**COME ON IN. (The painting is in the living room. I'm out back).**" Then she affixed clear tape along the upper edge of the paper and left it on the edge of the desk.

All of the items in the "before" list had been checked off. She was left with the "after" list. The thought of what came between made her heart thud in her chest. She felt nauseous. *This is ridiculous. You'll look as guilty as you feel. Calm down.* She tried lying down, but she was too nervous to nap. She poured herself a Riesling and went over the lists again. She could still take him to bed before killing him and claim rape, but that would probably result in a trial, and there would always be questions hanging over her. *Was she the instigator?* Howard would wonder what she was doing with the gun in the bedroom, when it should have been locked safely in his desk drawer. No, her plan was simple and only required proper timing. By the time she was through her second glass of wine, she felt a sense of calm inevitability. Either she would, or she wouldn't. She would just have to see how it played out, how all those intangibles would fall into place (or not). She couldn't anticipate all eventualities. She had done her very best. She had written her part. Now she would just have to play it.

She took the beach basket out to the far end of the pool and set it by the chaise lounge. Since Ramon had skipped his usual Tuesday visit to clean the pool, a profusion of purple jacaranda blossoms floated on the surface. She saw three dead bees, and another still struggling. It was close to the edge. She dipped her hand in the water and came up beneath it. It clung to her finger and she placed it on a basil leaf. It looked saturated. Evelyn had little hope it would recover.

Her garden tableau was still there — the hose, the shovel, the sun hat, the trowel, the gloves. She put on the hat and the gloves and picked up the trowel, wishing her life could be as simple and carefree as it was before Samantha had gone off to UCLA. She'd been living in ignorance, but she'd been happy. She began loosening the soil around the plants, pulling the weeds up with their roots, and deepening the furrows that would take the water. It didn't take her long to lose herself in the work, so it came as a surprise when she heard Ramon set down his case.

Evelyn turned and saw him. He was dressed uncharacteristically in khaki pants, a white, short-sleeved dress shirt, a narrow tie, and Florsheim loafers. He wore no hat or sunglasses. His hair had been oiled and neatly combed, and he held a laptop. It was as though he were going to a job interview. He wouldn't have dressed like this for her. He'd obviously preened and dressed to meet Howard, like one male bird posturing before another, jockeying for a position of power. Too bad Howard would never be here to see it. She smiled at him, serene in her role, not really believing she would go through with it.

She checked her watch. "You're early by three minutes."

"I want you and your husband to know you can count on me. I keep my appointments."

So far everything was going to plan. She felt as though she were playacting, watching her plans unfold as she had envisioned them, one step at a time. She could continue, or just let the time pass and not act.

"I see you brought your computer. Is the video on it?"

He handed her the laptop. "It's under photos."

She took off her right hand gardening glove so she could use the trackpad. It wasn't easy to see in the light of the afternoon sun, but she navigated the screen, found the video in question, and deleted it. "Is that it? Are there any more?"

"That's it; I swear."

135

She remembered the video of him massaging her back. Innocent enough, but it could be damning evidence in the right context. She found it and deleted it. She could still call it off now, if that were really all of the copies. Had she scrolled further back, she would have found videos of other women, but as it turned out, it was just as well she didn't.

"I have some spreadsheets on our investment, if you'd like to look."

"Not now," she said, placing the laptop on the chaise lounge. "Let me have your phone."

"You already deleted it from my phone."

"Let me have it anyway."

He handed it over. She opened the photo app and scrolled through the photos until she found the video of herself. She deleted it. That was the problem — the sad fact was that in a digital world, where copies could be made over and over again, there were never any guarantees.

"Okay, there, that's done," she said, and tossed the phone onto the chaise lounge, beside the laptop. "Howard won't be home for half an hour. You might as well clean the pool."

"Right."

She bent to retrieve her gardening glove and pulled it on. She still had time. She could wait. She could let the time pass and make excuses for Howard. She didn't have to rush into anything. Ramon went to his blue case and extracted the chemical analyzer. Seeing him standing there next to the pool brought to mind the last time they'd been here, how he'd held his phone above his head laughing at her. She remembered later fantasizing a different ending, rushing at him, shoulder down like a football linebacker. He would fall back and strike his head on the coping, and while he was unconscious she would roll his body into the water. Fantasies, of course, required too much luck. He knelt at the deep end and dipped a plastic beaker into the water to sample the chlorine and PH level. With his back turned, she realized this was the perfect moment. All she had to do was take off her gardening gloves, put on the latex gloves, retrieve the gun from the bottom of the bag, and shoot him. He took a dropper, withdrew a chemical from a small bottle, dripped one drop into the beaker, and shook it vigorously. She glanced at the beach basket, knowing that she was running out of time. Then, at the corner of her vision she saw the shovel. In two steps she had it in her hands. He slid a graduated color sample into a slot on the side of the beaker. She raised the shovel over her head like an axe. The shovel blade knocked some jacaranda blossoms loose. Ramon held the beaker up and tilted his head back to view the water's color against the sky, just as Evelyn brought the shovel down with all the force she could bring to bear. She knew that if she missed, he would retaliate. He would beat her and release the video online. She put her arms and her legs into it. With his chin tilted up, the curved backside of the blade came down squarely on top of his head. He pitched into the water like a sack of potatoes. Floating blossoms closed over the spot where he'd fallen in. The shaft vibrated in her hands.

Horrified at what she'd done, she was torn between jumping in after him or letting him drown. Her heart began to pound so hard she had to lean on the shovel just to keep from collapsing. She took several deep breaths until her heart slowed and her head cleared. Through the skein of blossoms she saw him touch the bottom on his back and bounce once, as if in slow motion. She thought she still had time to dive in and pull him to safety.

After almost a minute, a gush of bubbles boiled to the surface. His eyes jerked open in a panic, and she watched in terror as he gathered his legs beneath him and sprang off the bottom toward the air and oxygen. The crown of his head broke the surface just as the shovel came down upon it. He never got the chance to take another breath, but settled comatose toward the bottom. She watched, terrified, as though she'd had nothing to do with the matter. She watched him for a long time. When he aspirated water, his whole body spasmed, then suddenly relaxed, his mouth and eyes open as if in surprise. She dropped to her knees and shook. Nausea gripped her throat. She fought down the urge to vomit. She felt light-headed and faint, and knelt on the grass for what felt like five minutes. Then she replanted the shovel in the herb garden and hung her hat on it.

CHAPTER TWENTY-NINE

She took off the gardening gloves and dropped them into the beach basket, thinking, *The gloves will fit; they won't acquit.* She put on latex gloves and used the beach towel to wipe fingerprints from the laptop and phone. She checked her phone for the time, 6:03 p.m., and for Brooke (just leaving the gallery). She walked around the short hedge that hid the pool pump and heater and, after a moment's hesitation, changed the heater's target temperature from seventy-four to eighty-four degrees. In the warming water, the body would lose heat less quickly and push the estimated time of death later.

Studiously avoiding looking into the water, she set Ramon's phone conspicuously on the chaise lounge. *Don't think about it. If you don't think about it, it didn't really happen.* Next, she called Ramon's phone. It began playing Mozart's French horn rondo. When it went to voicemail she said, "Ramon, this is Evelyn Marsh — on Via Sueños Perdidos? I expected you Tuesday. The pool filter is full of jacaranda blossoms. Call me and let me know what's happening."

She put her phone in her pocket and slid the laptop into the beach bag and carried it around to the shallow end. There she left the beach towel and flip-flops. She carried the beach bag to the study, wiped off the Ruger and replaced it in the drawer. She checked Friend Finder. Brooke was already halfway there, perhaps twelve minutes away. She picked up the paper instructing Brooke to let herself in, and took it to the front door. She swung the door inward and taped the paper to the middle of the door, running her thumb over the tape to make it secure. As she began to close the door she glanced toward the driveway and froze. Ramon's truck stood parked in the driveway at the end of the front walk.

Her heart leaped into her throat. She'd completely forgotten about the truck. It was to avoid just this sort of contingency that she had planned and planned and gone over everything in her mind dozens of times. Now, when push came to shove, she'd come up short. She would have to move the truck, and she realized with horror that if the keys were in Ramon's pocket, she would have to dive for them, and she was running out of time. She sprinted to the truck in a panic, hoping against hope, jerked open the door and peered anxiously into the cab. With an enormous sense of relief, she saw the keys dangling from the ignition. There was no time to lose. She ran for the garage, opened the side door, hit the button to open the empty left bay where Howard parked his car, and ran back to the truck. The door had barely rotated up before she pulled into Howard's spot. She hit the button to close the door and sprinted for the house.

Breathless, she checked Friend Finder again. Brooke was less than five minutes away. She deleted Howard and Connie from her Friend Finder app. What next? She remembered Ramon's laptop in the beach basket in the study and decided there wasn't time to deal with it. She stripped down to her bikini, and dropped her halter top and cutoffs into the basket, and placed the basket at the foot of the stairs. Then she rushed through the dining room, hung her car keys on the hook in the kitchen, and turned off her phone and laid it on the kitchen counter. She peeled off the latex gloves and tossed them into the trash compactor. As she turned to go she remembered the list on the kitchen table. She picked it up. With no time to set a flame to it, she ran it under the faucet to blur the writing, then tore it into little pieces, and threw it on top of the gloves. She could hear Brooke's Honda Civic climbing the steep drive.

Evelyn exited through the French doors and jogged to the far end of the pool. She took a few deep breaths, composed her features, thought of Sam happily walking the streets of Paris, smiled, and turned to face the house. She resisted looking at the dark shape resting on the bottom of the pool. *No use crying over spilled milk. What's done is done.* Half a minute later, she saw Brooke come into the living room and stand before the easel.

Brooke studied the painting for a moment before glancing outside. She saw Evelyn, who waved before diving into the pool and swimming to the shallow end. She rose out of the water, bent for a towel, and stepped into flip-flops. She toweled off as she walked down the lawn. Brooke met her by the fountain. Evelyn beamed at her, genuinely glad for the release of tension that she'd felt for the last half hour.

"You have flowers in your hair," Brooke said and picked two off.

"Ah, the pool boy didn't come this week. The pool is thick with jacaranda blossoms." Evelyn sighed deeply. "Well, tell me, what do you think?" She nodded toward the painting.

"It's wonderful. It's not — and I don't mean this as a criticism of your other paintings — it's not as static, with the water flowing from the hose and the dog looking so expectant. I love the composition, and the mixed media gives it a textural interest."

"Do you think it's big enough?"

"It's perfect."

"I'm never sure what size best suits the subject. I guess now that we're digitizing them, I can print different sizes and make up my mind. Do you want help taking it out to your car."

"No, I've got it."

"Okay then, I'll just run upstairs and change."

She grabbed the beach bag on her way upstairs and tossed it into the corner of her closet. With her outfit already laid out, it took only a minute. She looked in the mirror, ran a brush through her damp hair, grabbed her purse and went downstairs with a light step. She met Brooke at the open trunk of her car.

"If it was any bigger, it wouldn't fit," Brooke said.

"Where should we go for dinner? Seafood or Mexican? I'm kind of in the mood for mussels, but I could go either way."

"Seafood is fine."

"Do you know the Beachside Cafe?"

"Next to Goleta Pier?"

"Right. The best way to get there from here is to turn right at the bottom of the drive, take Sueños Perdidos to Esperanza, Esperanza to Tranquila, then Tranquila to Mariposa." She pointed uphill. "Drive up to the garage. There's just room enough to turn around there."

Brooke did as instructed, as Evelyn went in the side door of the garage. A moment later, the door of the middle bay rolled up, and Evelyn backed out her white BMW. She pulled up behind Brooke's blue Civic, and tripped the remote to close the garage door. Then she got out of the car and approached Brooke's open window.

"I've got to close the French doors and lock up. You go ahead. I'll be right behind you." She repeated her directions and watched Brooke's Civic roll to the bottom of the drive and turn right. Then she drove the BMW a third of the way down the drive and parked. She ran back to the garage, opened the left bay, and backed Ramon's truck down to where the front walk intersected the driveway. There were several Taco Bell napkins on the passenger side seat, with which she hastily wiped the steering wheel, the shift lever, and the door handles. Then she jumped into the BMW and followed Brooke at a brisk pace. Rolling through a few stop signs, taking one shortcut, and accelerating through yellow lights, she arrived just as Brooke was getting out of her car.

"I don't know about you," Evelyn said, "but I'm looking forward to a nice cold glass of white wine."

Brooke was an engaging conversationalist, allowing natural tangents to dictate the subject matter, which distracted Evelyn from thinking about Ramon. Over dinner they talked of other restaurants, of Brooke's boyfriend, of framing art, and how a frame can affect how one sees a painting, or a view. "The same scene viewed through a rectangular window, seems somehow different from the same scene viewed through an arched window," Evelyn said. "It doesn't make a lot of sense, but it's true."

She told Brooke of her plans for the next painting. Eventually their colloquy drifted to travel, which brought to mind Samantha. "She's having such a fun time in Paris. Here, I'll show you where she's staying." Evelyn looked through her small purse. "Damn, I forgot my phone. I should call Howard; he won't know where I've gone. Can I borrow yours?" She got his voicemail, as expected. "Hi, Howie, I'm out to dinner with Brooke from the gallery. I forgot my phone, but don't worry about me. I'll be home around nine." She handed the phone back to Brooke. "Thanks. It's funny how dependent we are on these things. I remember the days when we only had landlines, and you never knew where anybody was. Now you know where everyone is twenty-four-seven. I don't know if that's such a good thing, but I've grown used to it."

Evelyn had two glasses of wine, which left her pleasantly tipsy and relaxed. "It's such a pleasure to have a night out without men," she said. "I love them, but the posturing and pontificating gets old. Or am I being unfair? Maybe it's just Howard."

No, Brooke assured her, it was all men. They couldn't help it. It's the way they established dominance. "They're a little bit like lions," Brooke said. "They don't do half the work, but they roar a lot and look important."

The two women, separated by age and experience, clinked glasses in solidarity and watched the sun sink into the Pacific.

CHAPTER THIRTY

In the parking lot Brooke said, "After we have the painting scanned, we'll go over some framing options. I have some ideas."

Evelyn smiled benignly, gave her a light hug and an air-kiss and said, "I had a wonderful time. We should do this more often."

The wine, the food, and the conversation left her feeling serene. If eventually she were found out, at least it wouldn't be tonight. Tonight she had an alibi.

She'd intended Howard to come home to an empty house, search for her, and discover the body. Of course, there was no guarantee he *would* search, in which case she would come home late and contrive to find the body in the morning before he went to work. But that was before she factored in the truck. The truck had changed everything. It would have been blocking the drive when Howard came home, as he usually did, around sunset. He would then have gone in search of the pool boy to complain. Had he looked into the pool? Had it been light enough to see? She hoped so. Of course, the keys were still in the ignition, so he could have just moved the truck, but surely he'd have looked for the owner. She fretted about the details all the way home, and even as she worried, she knew it was foolish because only one scenario would play out. She only had to play the cards that were dealt her.

Driving up Via Sueños Perdidos, she could see the glare of red and blue lights. She pulled to the curb opposite her drive, which was blocked by the truck, Howard's black BMW, and two police cars. An ambulance and sheriff's car were parked another forty feet up the road. The red lights of the ambulance and the "Christmas trees" atop the police and sheriff's cars lit the neighborhood in a garish glow.

Evelyn jumped from the car, leaving her door open, and ran up the drive. She was panting by the time she reached the front walk, where a police officer tried to stop her. She sidestepped him, crying, "I live here. What's happened? Where's my husband?" She managed to put breathless panic into her voice (it wasn't hard after running up the drive), and bolted into the house past one startled officer, down the hall to the living room, calling out, "Howard! Howard! Where's my husband? What's happened to my husband?"

Another officer at the French doors put up his hands. "Ma'am, please step outside. This is..."

"What's happened to my husband?"

Then she was outside and running toward people gathered around the pool. The pool lights were on, as well as police spotlights that lit up the poolside as bright as day and turned those who were backlit into faceless silhouettes. "Howard! Where's Howard?" she cried. She stopped in front of a black body bag. Her hands shot up to her face. "Howard!" she cried. "Oh, no!" For a moment, she almost believed it herself.

Then his voice spoke up from behind the bright lights. "Here, Evy. I'm over here."

She looked up dully, as if in a trance, then brightened. "Howard? Oh, Howard!"

She ran for him and hugged him tightly, burying her face in his chest. "I thought...Oh my god, I thought you were...Oh my. Who then?"

"The pool boy."

"How? What happened?"

A voice spoke up from behind her. "That's what we're trying to determine, ma'am. Could you tell me where you were for the past few hours?"

"Yeah, where were you?" Howard asked. "I tried calling, but you didn't answer."

"I left you a voicemail. I was at dinner with Brooke. I forgot my phone."

"Speaking of which," the sheriff said. "I'll need both your phones."

"Why?" Howard asked, a tone of belligerence creeping into his voice.

"We're authorized to impound anything that might be of material interest at the crime scene."

"What crime?"

"I should have said potential crime scene. A young man has died here under mysterious circumstances. It may have been an accident, but that remains to be seen. An autopsy will have to be performed. Now if you would please hand over your phones."

"I'm a lawyer. I know my rights."

"Then you'll know if you don't comply with my request, you'll be interfering with an officer in the performance of his duties."

"That's bullshit and you know it. If you want my phone, you need a warrant."

"Should I assume you have something to hide?"

"Don't think you can intimidate me. Come on, Evy, let's go inside."

"You're not going anywhere," the officer said.

"You can't hold me."

"I can, and I will. Would you like to come down to the station for questioning?" The officer then turned to the sheriff. "How fast can we get a warrant?"

"Hold on, hold on," Howard said. "Okay, all right. No need to get adversarial here. I'm on your side." Grumbling, he pulled a phone from his coat pocket and handed it over.

"And your phone, ma'am?"

"I must have left it inside. I don't know where."

"We'll find it. Now, if you'd answer a few questions."

146

CHAPTER THIRTY-ONE

The area around the pool was cordoned off with yellow crime scene tape, and motion detectors were set in place. The police and sheriff didn't leave until well after midnight, with the admonition to stay out of the backyard and to call them immediately if either of them saw or heard anything out-of-the-ordinary.

Neither Evelyn nor Howard had much to say.

"That poor boy," Evelyn remarked. "I wonder what could have happened. Do you really think he might have been murdered?"

"No, how could it be? He probably just slipped and hit his head. I just don't understand why he was here in the first place. It was too late in the day to be cleaning pools. And he was wearing a tie, for Christ's sake. It's just strange."

Howard made himself a martini to calm his nerves. "You want one?" he asked.

"No, I'm going to take a warm shower and a sleeping pill."

Howard set his briefcase on the kitchen table, popped open the latch, and took out his cell phone.

"I thought you gave your phone to the police."

"I gave them *a* phone."

"Whose phone was it then?"

"Yours. You left it on the chaise lounge."

Evelyn smiled smugly. "How very clever."

"I thought so."

"But won't you get in trouble?"

"I don't see how. I remember very clearly, he said, 'If you have a cell phone, hand it over.' I did. Anyway, I have a fiduciary duty to my clients. I've got confidential correspondence on my phone. Doesn't matter though. It'll all be a moot point as soon as they realize the boy just had an accident.

"I suppose so," Evelyn said.

They both awoke groggy and exhausted. Evelyn made coffee, while Howard took a shower. He was half an hour late leaving for work.

As soon as he was gone, Evelyn dressed and carried the beach bag to the garage. She put her gardening gloves in a bin with trowels and spades and weeders and gardening shears. Then she backed her BMW out of the garage, placed the beach bag under the left rear tire, and backed over it. The computer made a satisfying crunching sound. She put the bag on the passenger seat and drove down the hill to the Hope Ranch Private Beach, careful to check that no one was following. There was a restroom at the parking lot. Anyone seeing her enter the restroom would have seen her go in with a beach bag, and come out a minute later with a beach bag. The crushed laptop had been stuffed into the trash can and covered with paper towels. She took off her sandals and walked at the edge of the water, letting the sound of the surf wash over her and ease her fears.

Back home, she went online to search for pool services, and left messages with two to call her back. Later that afternoon, she sat at the dining room table, sketching. The concept was coming into focus now: an open suitcase on a bed; men's clothes, neatly folded, but no suit, suggesting this trip was of a personal nature (for pleasure or of necessity had yet to be determined). Reflected in a mirror above the chest of drawers, an open doorway revealed a pedestal sink, above which a fogged mirror reflected the indistinct silhouette of a man.

While she contemplated how to infer the nature of the trip, a white SUV with a gold emblem on the door came up the drive, followed by a white and blue police cruiser. Her heart beat just a trifle faster. She knew she had done everything in her power to provide herself with an alibi, but she also knew from watching CSI dramas on television that scientists in the crime lab would eventually ferret out the guilty party. She was resigned that if that time came, she would go meekly to prison. However, until that strand of hair, swab of DNA, or fingerprint linked her to the crime, she would play the part of the innocent bystander. She was ready when they knocked on the door.

There were three men, a thick, blond patrolman in uniform, who couldn't have been much older than her son, and two middle-aged men wearing short-waisted navy-blue jackets with logos that identified them as investigators from the office of the coroner. The eldest, in his forties, looked tired and apologetic as he held up a sheet of paper. "We have a search warrant," he said. She didn't bother to confirm it; she expected it.

"Do you know what happened to that poor young man?" she asked as she opened the door wide to admit them.

"That's what we're trying to determine, ma'am. I'm Detective Olson. This is Detective Marks. We'll be handling the investigation."

"You weren't here last night."

"No, ma'am. We've been brought in to answer some questions that remain unanswered."

"Such as?"

"First, do you have any computers or tablets on the premises?"

"In the study," she said, flicking her eyes to the open door, through which the computer was plainly visible on the desk.

"Our computer forensics team will want to look it over."

"What could a computer in our study have to do with that boy's accident?"

"It remains to be seen if it was an accident."

Evelyn turned a dismayed look upon each of them. "You don't think it was an accident then?"

149

"That's what we're trying to determine. The autopsy revealed some anomalies we'd like to clear up."

Evelyn shrugged. "Whatever I can do to help. But last night they took our phones, and now you're taking our computer. How am I supposed to contact my daughter? She's in Europe. How can I text or email her without a phone or computer?"

"I'm sorry, but an investigation of this sort takes precedence. The phones and computer will remain in our custody until the investigation is over."

The patrolman went to the study, while Detective Marks left to examine the scene of death in daylight.

"Now, if you can tell me, when was the last time you saw Ramon Esposito?"

"The Tuesday before last, I suppose. But I didn't always see him when he came to service the pool."

"Was Tuesday his usual day?"

"Yes, although he didn't come this Tuesday, which is why I called him yesterday."

"At what time?"

"Well, it had to be before my friend came over. She arrived around six thirty. You know I gave a statement last night."

"Let's go over it again. Maybe you'll remember something you forgot."

"As I said…"

He was good-looking, in a rugged sort of way, in his midforties, with a sprinkling of salt-and-pepper in his hair and a furrowed brow. He had green eyes and a soothing, world-weary voice, and she couldn't help but notice that he wore no wedding band. She supposed it was the job. It would be hard for a homicide detective to leave his cares at work, or to have a positive outlook on life.

Howard came home early in a foul mood, livid that the authorities had impounded his phone, his laptop and his office computer. "I'll sue the assholes," he ranted. "This is costing me money. How am I supposed to work without a computer?"

"I asked them the very same thing this afternoon when they took the computer from the study."

"What?! When? You didn't tell me they were here."

"How could I? They took our phones."

"What the hell? What do they think they'll find, for Christ's sake?"

Evelyn knew what they *wouldn't* find. They wouldn't find any browser history pointing to forensic investigation, because she'd confined her searches to the public library. "Could you ask them for our phones?" she asked. "We can't get along without phones. Sam won't be able to get in touch with us."

"I'll look into it tomorrow. What else did they take?"

"The shovel, a trowel. I don't know; there's a list."

"What did they say? What reason did they give?"

"They didn't say."

"And you just let them?"

"Of course, they're the police."

"Did they have a search warrant?"

"Yes, of course; I'm not stupid."

Howard looked up at the ceiling and heaved a sigh. "Why couldn't the son of a bitch die in somebody else's backyard?"

S.W. CLEMENS

CHAPTER THIRTY-TWO

On the weekend, they went shopping together for the first time in years. They bought new phones and two laptops, one for the study and one for Howard's office. Evelyn downloaded the Friend Finder app and texted Samantha: "I don't want to alarm you, but you should know that the pool boy drowned in our pool. The police have been a nuisance. They took our phones and computer, so please send me all your contact info again. Hope you're having a grand time in Paris. Love, Mom."

Though she knew it unlikely, for a week or two Evelyn worried that the crushed laptop might have been found in the trash and turned over to the police. It was the only thing that had been in her control that might link her to the crime. Of course, she had no control over what the detectives might find in Ramon's apartment or in his truck. If he'd kept an appointment book noting their Thursday meeting, she was sunk. So she was on tenterhooks when Detective Olson came back unannounced.

She was in the living room by the open French doors, dressed in her painter's smock and working on a study of the painting she was calling *Coming or Going?* In her own mind, the answer was still ambiguous. The study was on the small side (nine by twelve), in oil pastels. The final would be larger (eighteen by twenty-four) in oil paint, but she was undecided whether to make it dark or light, and whether to include an open window, or not. The knock on the front door made her stomach do a flip-flop, and she wondered with trepidation if she were about to be arrested. Howard would post bail, she thought, so chances were she would have time to finish the painting before trial.

She answered the door and invited the detective in.

152

"I didn't know you were an artist," Olson said, observing her smock and the pastel she held in her hand.

She was tempted to answer, as she had most of her life, that it was just a hobby. But that had changed. So she simply said, "Aspiring. You can find a few of my things at The Whitfield Gallery."

Olson nodded his head as a dawning comprehension lit his eyes. "I know it. I was there just a few days ago."

The admission didn't really surprise her. Someone surely would have interviewed Brooke to confirm her alibi.

"What can I do for you?"

"I've come to look at the scene again, to get a few things straight for my report."

"Feel free," Evelyn said. She escorted him toward the back of the house. "Are you going to take the tape down soon? I'd like to use my pool again before summer is over."

"I think that can be arranged. I'll be just a minute."

Evelyn made a pretense of working, while watching as he paused by the chaise lounge. He stood erect, then bent his head, looking from his phone's tiny screen to the neighbor's hedge. He took photos, then walked over to the palm and reached out to touch the trunk. With a frisson of fear, she knew he'd seen the hole. Would he know it for what it was? Did it matter? A minute later he returned. She added a line of color to her study and smudged it with her thumb.

"Thank you," he said, "that was helpful." He swiveled around, taking in the whole room. "This is a wonderful old house. Is that yours?" he asked, indicating the painting over the fireplace.

"Yes." It was a painting of a bucket, a fish head, and a fishing pole leaning against the railing at the end of Stearns Wharf. Between the railing and the horizon, a sailboat plied a whitecapped sea.

He stepped over to the fireplace to get a closer look at the painting. "It's terrific. You're very good."

153

Evelyn brushed off her hands. "Thank you. Is there anything else?"

His gaze had wandered to the framed photos on the mantelpiece below the painting. "This looks familiar. Is it the Big Island?"

"Maui."

"Lahaina, right? Do your children still live at home?"

"My son works in LA. My daughter goes to UCLA, but she's traveling."

"That's right, I remember — you said she was in Paris?"

"For the summer."

"When did she leave?"

Evelyn felt an icy hand grip her insides. What did he suspect? What did he know? "She's been gone about a month."

"When will she be coming back?"

"I'm not sure. The fall quarter starts in mid-September."

"Can I take a picture of your painting? I'd like to show my partner."

Her intestines began to cramp. "Be my guest."

He spent a minute ostensibly composing a shot of the painting, though she suspected it was a ruse to take a photo of the family portrait, and she had a sick feeling she knew why.

"Is that it?" she said. "I'd like to get back to my work."

"I have just a few more questions." He took out a notebook and pen. "It's not exactly high tech, but I find it helps me think." He held up his phone and said, "I'd also like to record this, if I may, just for backup, in case my notes aren't clear."

"Aren't you supposed to read me my rights?"

Olson looked genuinely surprised. "I'm not arresting you. I'm just gathering facts for my investigation. We don't read you your rights unless you're a suspect or in custody. Of course, if you refuse to answer my questions and ask me to leave, I'd have to ask myself why, if you have nothing to hide."

Evelyn sat down on the couch. "I'll give you five minutes."

154

"Very well. How long was Ramon Esposito in your employ?"

"Let's see. Mario retired in May, so it must have been May. I don't know when exactly. I'll have a record of it in my checkbook, if you'd like the exact date."

"I would, but it can wait. Do you remember who referred him?"

The detective may have run over his time, but Evelyn didn't really mind. He had a pleasant voice and a chatty, conversational manner. When he asked about Ramon, she substituted an image of Mario, a largely invisible individual who came and went without drawing attention to himself. There was no need to lie or make anything up. It was more a matter of leaving certain things out. The questions, which seemed inconsequential to Evelyn, were helping to build a picture in Olson's mind. Some questions opened doors, some closed them, but all the while the picture was taking shape and clarity.

The detectives came a few more times, first Olson, then Marks, and once together. None of their questions seemed particularly relevant. The police had no motive to hang their case on. The familiar motives — cuckolded husband; business deal gone sour — didn't hold water. The police could show no connection between the men. Connie would provide Howard with his alibi. So despite their suspicions, with nothing more to go on, it was still possible the death would be ruled accidental.

She began to think they'd all gotten away scot-free. The more she thought about it (and she thought about little else), the more convinced she became that she was in the clear. Her alibi was impregnable. She was beyond the reach of authorities.

Still, given her culpability, an objective observer might expect her to feel the prick of conscience, a twinge of guilt. And here that observer would be surprised, for with each passing day she began to think the whole sordid business with Ramon was just a bad dream, an aberration in her otherwise orderly life. She could almost believe she hadn't done it. She could almost believe that Howard was the guilty party (and he *was* guilty, of course...of adultery). No, she hadn't slept with that young man (of her own free will) and, she told herself, she hadn't killed him. That wasn't how she saw herself. Who would say she was capable? Who would accuse her? Ramon had had an accident, that's all, a simple accident. She wasn't a murderer.

And then she thought of that poor gopher, and she knew otherwise. She felt bad about the gopher. She didn't feel so bad about Ramon who, after all, had chosen his fate. She had no compunction about stopping him and his wicked ways. It was unfortunate, but when pushed to the edge of a cliff, it was perfectly acceptable to defend oneself. As she saw it, she'd had no choice. And if society held that self-preservation was no defense, she didn't agree.

The following days were quiet, if not carefree. The police tape was removed, and she went back to her routine of gardening in the morning, followed by a swim and long hours spent reading. She switched from mysteries to historical romances. In the afternoons, she worked on her business plan or painted, as the mood struck her.

Evelyn's nights were less sanguine. Howard was even more silent than usual, and carried an air of anxiety and barely contained anger. On days when the detectives questioned him at work, he would come home grousing about the incompetence of the police, and how he was being hounded by innuendos and false assumptions.

"Goddamn it, I'm innocent," he declared one night over a second martini.

"I know, I know," Evelyn said in a tone that meant, *There, there, honey, don't you worry.* "I know you are. They'll realize it soon enough."

156

"They're just frustrated. They want someone to take the blame. It was just a goddamn accident. I can't help it if the guy slipped. Whose fault is that? Nobody's."

Samantha came home on the first of September, happier and more worldly than when she'd left. For ten short days, she brought life back into the house. Evelyn monopolized her time, taking vicarious pleasure as her daughter related the summer's adventures with breathless enthusiasm. They went shopping and to lunch, and visited the grandparents. Evelyn had just gotten used to having her around again, when it was time to move her into her new apartment in Westwood.

To his credit, Howard took a full day to help with the move. He put on a brave face, trying hard not to share his sullen mood. Robert and his girlfriend also made an appearance, and they all went out to dinner at a Thai restaurant near the campus.

Later, on the way home, the conversation naturally turned toward the children. Howard was as relaxed as she'd seen him in a year. It was almost like old times, and she reminded herself that he'd been a decent husband (so far as she knew) for most of their marriage. She wished she had a positive opinion of him now, but his infidelities and constant lying had undermined what esteem she'd had for him. Now, listening to Howard talk about his hopes for their children, she thought she could almost forgive him, but she didn't think she could live with him.

A week later, Howard was arrested at his office, charged with Voluntary Manslaughter.

CHAPTER THIRTY-THREE

Later he came to her quite over the limit, his speech slurred with gin. "Honey? Evy? You know, I didn't kill that goddamn pool boy, but...well, you know I'm not perfect. They'll try to drag me through the mud and...I'd rather you didn't sit through the trial."

"How would that look? If your own wife isn't there to support you? How would that look?"

"Just the same, I'd rather you didn't come to court."

"I'm sorry, but I don't have a choice. I've been served a subpoena; I'm a witness. I have to be there."

"But on days when you're not needed...."

"I could be called on anytime."

Howard looked around as if confused. "I just...I'm sorry, Evy."

He was so pitiful that Evelyn felt compelled to comfort him, until she remembered, *Come and get it!* Then her heart hardened.

Howard was more annoyed than worried. He retained his partner to present the defense.

"The judge wouldn't allow a Preliminary Hearing," Albert Katz Jr. said, "because you're too high profile. They have to show that no one is above the law, not even lawyers. So she's sending it to the Grand Jury, which means we can't tell our side unless it goes to trial. I'll do what I can, but you haven't given me much to work with."

"There's nothing to give; it's total BS," Howard told him confidently. "I don't know what they think they're going to prove, because I didn't do anything. I never even met the man. Evy hired him."

When the Grand Jury handed down its indictment, Howard was baffled. "Why would I possibly want to kill the pool boy? What motive would I have?"

"That's what we'll find out, as soon as I file a Motion of Discovery."

The first thing Katz saw, when the inventory of evidence was turned over, was the list of witnesses. He stormed into Howard's office and slapped down the report on his desk. "Why does my ex-wife show up as a witness for the prosecution?"

Howard blanched. "Shit," he said. He picked up the file and looked at the witness list. Also listed as witnesses for the prosecution were Brooke Bass, Evelyn Marsh, and Samantha Marsh. "What the fuck is this?"

"You tell *me.*"

Howard pursed his lips, staring at the names, his heart hammering in his chest. "We may need to call Connie as a witness for the defense, too."

"What the hell have you done?"

"Sorry, I didn't want to bring her into this."

"I'll have to withdraw from the case, of course. It's a conflict of interest. I'll fix you up with Donald LeMay. He's competent." Albert stared at him until their eyes met. "Tell me you didn't do it."

"I didn't, I swear."

That Howard and his paramour were quits, was evident by his actually going to the gym on Tuesdays and Thursdays. Exercise seemed the only thing that relieved his stress, and Evelyn was happy to have him out of the house, for his company had become almost intolerable, their conversations fraught with tension. If she asked about the case, he offered noncommittal answers.

"I don't like being kept in the dark," she'd say.

"It's nothing for you to be concerned about," he'd say.

"Nothing to be concerned about? Are you crazy?"

"I don't want to talk about it."

And so it went, 'round and 'round, until the day she got an hysterical call from Samantha.

"Mom, I've just been served with a subpoena to testify against Daddy!"

Evelyn's heart sank. "Did they say about what?"

"No, it's just an order to appear. I don't understand; I wasn't even here."

It could only be about one thing, the only thing that could provide a motive, and Evelyn couldn't tell her daughter she knew.

"Mom?"

"Yes?" she asked in a whisper.

"Do I have to?"

"Yes, Sweetie, I believe you do. Can you excuse me a minute? I'll be right back."

Evelyn ran for bathroom and threw up.

That evening when Howard came home, they had a row. "When were you going to tell me our daughter has been called as a witness?" Evelyn asked furiously. "How long have you known?"

"I thought maybe they were bluffing. I can't imagine what they think Sam could know. She was in Paris, for gods' sakes. It can't be important."

Evelyn sat in the first row behind her husband, squirming from time to time with the discomfort of the hard, wooden seat. She tried to look engaged; she was being observed, after all, but it was impossible — she was bored with the endless repetition of questions directed at each potential juror during the selection process.

Nonetheless, she was curious to know what the Grand Jury had seen to persuade them to indict Howard. She didn't see how he could be connected to the murder weapon — she hadn't used his gun as she'd intended. And there could be no evidence connecting *her* to the murder weapon, as there would be no fingerprints. She'd worn gloves. Her worries were all reserved for Samantha. The only saving grace was that Santa Barbara's newspapers were so small that Samantha's shame would garner less exposure over the course of the trial than internet porn sites garnered in a day, and newspaper coverage would wane as the next story took precedence.

The direction of the prosecution's strategy was made apparent when Judge Sharon White asked several questions to determine the impartiality of the jurors. Howard was sitting at a table with his attorney, looking decidedly bored as the judge reminded the prospective jurors of their duty, defined Voluntary Manslaughter, and questioned each about his or her ability to remain unbiased in such a case. She then went on to ask general and pointed questions about pornography. At which point Howard perked up and LeMay leaned in urgently for a *sotto voce* conference. Howard shook his head and raised his hands palms upward in an exaggerated shrug, making it abundantly clear to all in the courtroom that he was as confused as this lawyer.

Robert announced that he would take a few days off work to attend and show his support. Evelyn quickly talked him out of it. "They're going to drag your father through the mud, and he doesn't want you to witness it. Please respect his wishes." After a halfhearted counterargument, Robert reluctantly conceded. Samantha's appearance at the trial was scheduled for the second day.

The trial began the first week of February. Gerard Roper rose from the prosecution table and approached the jury box.

He rested his chin on steepled fingers and looked at a spot above the jurors' heads, letting the pause give weight to his words. Then he scanned the twelve men and women, and began.

"A young man is dead. Ramon Esposito, just twenty-nine years of age, born in Argentina, a naturalized US citizen who came here as an infant with his family seeking a better life. He excelled at school, won a scholarship to college, and started his own company. He surely had dreams. Dreams like any other man, of falling in love, of starting a family of his own, of building a business. But all of those dreams came to an end when his life was brutally taken from him. When a life is taken, it not only robs the victim of his future, it robs society of his particular contribution. We will never know what potential he may have had. He never had the chance to show it. We cannot bring him back to life, but we can seek justice.

"We don't know all of the facts that led to his murder. The only one who knows for certain is his murderer." Roper paused here to turn and look admonishingly at Howard for a moment before continuing. "We do know for certain that on the evening of August sixth Ramon Esposito drowned in the pool belonging to the defendant, at Eighteen Via Sueños Perdidos."

Evelyn, who had been playing the meek and loyal wife, perked up at these words. *The house does not belong to the defendant. It belongs to me,* she thought.

Roper thrust his hands in his pockets and rocked on his heels. "So aptly named. *Sueños Perdidos* — Lost Dreams. Ramon Esposito lost his dream of a future that night. But was this a ghastly accident? No, this was murder. The defendant would have you believe that he returned home after a long day's work, and found the body of the victim at the bottom of his pool. It's true that drowning was the actual cause of death, but the prosecution will present evidence showing that Ramon Esposito was struck with a blunt instrument with enough force to fracture his skull. We will prove, beyond a reasonable doubt, that the defendant was present, that he had motive, and that he wielded the instrument of death.

"Motive. You heard the judge define Voluntary Manslaughter, the offense with which the defendant is charged. We believe that a worse crime may have been committed, involving premeditation, but the law requires we prove that the defendant is guilty *beyond a reasonable doubt.* In a case where there is only one eyewitness to the crime — the murderer himself — we must make inferences from the facts that are known, and what we do know, without a doubt, is that the victim possessed the means to provoke the defendant to strike in the heat of passion. When you learn what those means were, you may find yourself sympathizing with the defendant. But remember that no man is above the law, no matter the provocation, no matter his station in life. No man has the right to take another's life, to steal decades of experience, the promise of a life. The victim may have acted rashly, may have made errors of judgement, or even been morally reprehensible." Roper paused to let the words sink in. "But that doesn't justify taking his life. The defendant had recourse under the law, as he well knew. He is an officer of the court, after all. He is supposed to uphold the law. And he will be judged under the law, the same as anyone else, high or low in our society."

CHAPTER THIRTY-FOUR

Despite her protestations, the first day of the trial Evelyn's parents insisted on sitting with her to lend their emotional support. Brooke sat on her other side.

"How are you holding up?" Brooke asked.

Evelyn smiled benignly. "Fine, I'm not worried. I know he's innocent."

Brooke looked at her with just a hint of awe. "You're a good person, Evelyn, a really good person."

If only you knew, Evelyn thought, doing her best impression of Mona Lisa.

Evelyn and Brooke were the first to take the stand to establish the timeline.

As subsequent testimony unfolded, Evelyn had to suppress a smile, for despite her careful planning to establish an alibi, it was the thing she hadn't counted on that saved her bacon. The truck blocking the drive placed her above suspicion, for it proved that Ramon had arrived after the women left for dinner at six thirty, and before Howard returned home. It was pure serendipity.

The Coroner testified, "On the night in question, the pool heater kept cycling on and off, so it's impossible to know for certain the temperature of the water when the victim drowned, which makes estimating the time of death based solely on heat loss problematic. However, knowing that the deceased was still alive as of six thirty, and knowing that the police were called at eight thirty, combined with the body and water temperature at the time of discovery, we can extrapolate a fairly precise time of death at seven forty-five p.m., give or take forty-five minutes. So, as early as seven, or as late as eight thirty."

He then related the findings of the autopsy, the cause of death (drowning), and the contributing factor (fractured skull).

Detective Olson testified that the victim had been struck on the head with a blunt object, and that grains of soil were imbedded in the scalp, consistent with the shovel that was found not ten feet from the pool. "Based on the fact that the victim was struck twice on the crown of his head, the individual who struck the blows must have been at least six-feet tall."

When Connie was called to the stand by the prosecution, she looked to Evelyn with a half apologetic smirk and a shrug of the shoulders that spoke volumes. Evelyn interpreted these expressions as the nonverbal equivalent of "Sorry, but if you can't keep your man satisfied, what'd you expect? Anyway, I didn't think I'd get caught, so it's not like I did it to hurt you."

Roper asked her simply, without embellishment, if Howard had been at her house that evening, and when he had left. "He was with me from five twenty, to eight."

"How can you be so sure of the time?"

"Well, he always came after five, and he always left about eight, so he could get home by eight twenty. It's a twenty-minute drive."

"He was in the habit of visiting you?"

"Tuesdays and Thursdays, after work."

Howard hung his head and seemed to shrink into his suit coat.

Brooke leaned toward Evelyn. "I'm so sorry you had to find out this way. I wanted to tell you."

"You called. 'When the cat's away'?"

"Yeah."

Evelyn patted her on the knee. "I thought Howard was the cat."

Meanwhile, Bill Hightower was glaring menacingly at the back of Howard's head.

Marjorie grasped Evelyn's right hand. "Let's go!"

165

Evelyn felt that every eye in the courtroom was on her, as though she were a player in a drama. She'd been assigned the part of the wronged and suffering wife. She'd played the part privately for several months now, had been resigned to it, but she was surprised how much more it stung to play before an audience. Private humiliation was bad enough. Public humiliation was magnified by each pair of eyes upon her. She knew they were all judging her, comparing her to the mistress, measuring her shortcomings as a wife.

"Yes, let's go," she said.

Evelyn stood tight-lipped, and she and her parents walked up the aisle without looking to the left or the right as they exited the courtroom.

"Come home with us," her mother said.

"And let him chase me from my house? No, uh uh. He can move in with his mistress."

"Are you sure?" her father asked. "It might be good to get away."

"Not now. Maybe later. You two go on home now. I'd like some time alone."

In the car on the way home from court, Howard looked contrite. The guilty often look contrite when they're caught. But the shame he felt was less for what he'd done than for being found out.

"I want you out of the house," Evelyn said firmly.

"Is that such a good idea? What about Robbie and Sam?"

"They're adults. They'll understand."

"What if I don't want to go? I'm sorry, okay? I know I screwed up."

"You screwed *some*thing. Some*body*."

"What can I say? I'm weak; I admit it. I apologize. Anyway, it's over."

"I don't care if it's over. It's not about where you put your prick. It's about trust. I can't trust you anymore, Howard, can't believe anything you say. You've been lying to me for a year. You can sleep in Robert's old room until you find a place to stay. With any luck, the state will have a cell for you shortly."

"Now, Evy, don't be that way."

"And don't call me Evy!"

CHAPTER THIRTY-FIVE

After they returned home, Evelyn locked herself in her bedroom and called Samantha. "Sweetie, I have some bad news, and I don't know how to tell you other than to just tell it like it is. I'm afraid your father has been having an affair."

"No! Not Daddy!"

"Yes, he and Connie Katz — Connie Whitfield? The lady who's been selling my paintings."

"Oh, Mom, that's just awful" There was a long silence. "I'm so sorry. How awful for you. Is there anything I can do?"

"Just send love and hugs. It's a rotten thing, but we'll muddle through. You're coming to court tomorrow?"

"I have to."

"We'll just have to grin and bear it together."

The next morning, Howard said, "Come on, we'll be late for court."

"I don't think we should drive together. You take your car. I'll follow later."

"Oh, Evy — Evelyn, I don't think that's such a good idea."

"Just go."

Evelyn had dreaded the day Samantha would take the stand and the video would be revealed. For days, she'd worried over how the revelations would be handled in the press, and how it would affect Samantha. She needn't have worried at all, as Judge Sharon White cleared the courtroom of all but the jury and witnesses. Samantha sat with Evelyn.

Detective Marks was the first to take the stand.

The prosecution passed out still photos to the judge, the jury and Marks. Roper asked, "Detective Marks, do you recognize this photo?"

"Yes, this is a still from a video we found in the victim's apartment."

"Can you elaborate?"

"Sure, when we searched the victim's apartment, we found several flash drives containing..." Marks cleared his throat, "...what appear to be homemade pornographic videos."

"Could you identify the subjects of the videos?"

"Of the four females in question, we were able to identify two. The male in each appears to be the victim, Ramon Esposito."

"And were you able to identify the woman in this still shot?"

"That would be Constance Whitfield, also known as Constance Katz."

Next, Connie took the stand. Roper asked if she had consented to be videoed.

"No, he used a hidden camera."

"And did he use the video to extort money from you?"

"Well, he tried, but I..."

"Did he threaten to post the video online if you didn't pay?"

"He tried, but I called his bluff. I mean...there are worse things than being called a cougar. Anyway, he didn't do himself any favors in that video. It was very short, if you know what I mean," she said, winking at the prosecutor.

"By short, you mean...?"

"In length." There was tittering among the jurors, and she realized her error. "I mean it didn't last long."

Evelyn thought, *Is this the same stud we're talking about? Short? She must be a witch in bed.*

"Did he say what he wanted money for?"

"He had some business scheme he wanted me to invest in."

Samantha listened with dawning horror as Connie testified. Now she knew why she'd been called. She hung her head and hid behind a veil of hair, feeling utter humiliation. "Oh god, Mom. I'm so sorry."

"It's not your fault."

The prosecutor introduced more photos and another flash drive with video into evidence and called Samantha to the stand. She testified that yes, she was the woman in the still shots taken from that video. No, she had not consented to being videoed. No, he had not tried to extort money from her using the video as leverage.

Evelyn was grateful for a female judge, who had enough discretion to resist playing the entire video in court.

Despite the introduction of a motive, there was no obvious connection — no smoking gun, no demand for blackmail, no phone calls, no money trail connecting Howard to Ramon. No gun as she'd planned. It was all supposition. *If* Ramon had shown Howard the video, or *if* he somehow knew of Howard's dalliance with Connie and *if* he had demanded blackmail as a result, only then could a motive be established, and there was no proof of either. Evelyn didn't see how they could convict him on the evidence.

That is, until the shovel was brought into the picture. The forensic pathologist testified that grains of soil had been forced into the scalp as the victim was struck twice with a blunt instrument that conformed to the shovel found at the scene of the murder. He'd been struck with enough force to fracture the skull. Could the blow have killed him? Possibly. And it would have contributed to the victim drowning.

Moreover, he'd been struck on the crown of the head, indicating that the assailant must have been a tall man. Evelyn saw how the pathologist could come to that conclusion. It made sense if Ramon had been standing, though she knew he'd been kneeling at the edge of the pool, head tilted back to view a beaker of water against the sky.

Furthermore, the pathologist went on, the defendant had left patent fingerprints in his own blood on the shaft of the shovel. At this revelation, Evelyn sat up at attention. Howard looked aghast at his lawyer. Evelyn was completely alert and more than a little perplexed. That her own fingerprints had not been found was no surprise, as she'd been wearing gardening gloves. But how the devil did Howard's prints get on the shovel? And in his own blood. She couldn't imagine. Two months would pass before she remembered the incident of the previous spring, when Howard had pricked his fingers on the rosebush on the day of her first murder.

The prosecutor's closing statement was short and to the point, and it might have been true. He laid out the salient facts as they were known through testimony and forensic evidence. They knew, by the testimonies of Mrs. Marsh and Ms. Bass, that Ramon had not yet arrived by the time they left for the restaurant at approximately 6:40 p.m. Ramon's truck was blocking the driveway when Mr. Marsh returned home at approximately 8:20 p.m. Curiously, though evidence suggested he had been testing the water shortly before the assault (paraphernalia was found in the pool, and his kit was nearby), Ramon's dress was more in keeping with a business meeting. The only fingerprints on Ramon's smartphone were those of the defendant.

"He would have you believe he just happened to pick it up at the scene before he found the body."

The prosecutor then went on to recount that the phone contained pornographic videos, including one of the defendant's mistress. This, along with a flash drive in the victim's possession that contained a compromising video of the defendant's daughter, and the fact that the victim had previously tried to extort money from the defendant's mistress, suggested that the victim may have shown the defendant such a video in an attempt at extortion, giving the defendant more than enough motive to lash out in anger.

"We contend that confronted with this material, Howard Marsh flew into a rage, grabbed the nearest weapon, a shovel, and twice hit Ramon Esposito with enough force to fracture his skull. Whether the victim fell into the pool or was pushed may be inconclusive, but there is no doubt that Ramon Esposito then drowned."

Evelyn nodded. Yes, that was the most plausible conclusion.

"No man, not even an officer of the court, is above the law. Therefore, we ask this jury to return a verdict of guilty as charged."

CHAPTER THIRTY-SIX

The jury took nearly two hours to deliberate, implying there was some dissension, but in the end the foreman handed down a guilty verdict. Howard turned to his attorney, loudly protesting, "But I didn't do it!" Donald LeMay patted Howard on the back, shook his head, and shrugged. Howard, humiliated and chastened by all that had happened, gave only a furtive glance in Evelyn's direction before the bailiff led him out of the courtroom by a side door.

Evelyn considered his situation. She had only done what he should have done to protect their daughter, and if one of them had to pay, it was only right that that person should be Howard. She didn't feel she owed him any loyalty, given the circumstances. Her only regret was the effect it would have on Sam. Poor Sam. Evelyn turned on her phone and texted: "Dearest Sam, so sorry to report your father was found guilty today. Sentencing is next Wednesday. Be brave. Don't let this deter you from your studies."

Nonetheless, Samantha came home that evening. "I can't believe it," she said, holding back tears. "First that awful lady, now this."

Evelyn poured them both a glass of Riesling. She clinked her glass against Sam's. "Just you and me, kid."

"How could Daddy do that? It's all my fault. If I hadn't had sex with that pool boy…."

"No, you can't think like that. You father knows right from wrong. He knew better. And it might not have been about you anyway. It might have been about Connie Katz. We don't know."

The front door slammed shut, and a moment later Robert appeared in the kitchen. "When were you going to tell me? I got an email from Nate Nelson, or I wouldn't know!"

"I'm sorry. I've been so discombobulated. I would've called in the morning, but there's nothing for you to do," Evelyn said.

"I can be here for you. Do you really think he's guilty?"

"The evidence would have it appear so."

"Why? Why did he do it?"

"I'd rather spare you the sordid details," Evelyn said, glancing sideways at her daughter with a look that invited confidence.

Robert shook his head in disbelief. "It's unbelievable."

"Believe it or not, your father is going to prison."

In the hall of the courthouse before sentencing, Evelyn overheard Detective Olson tell a colleague, "This was an easy one, as most crimes of passion are. There isn't time to cover your tracks, and Marsh was careless."

Howard's protestations of innocence notwithstanding, he was convicted of Voluntary Manslaughter and sentenced to three years in Soledad State Prison. Evelyn thought three years was just about right for him to reflect on the error of his ways.

CHAPTER THIRTY-SEVEN

And that was how Evelyn managed to get away with her
second murder, which was *not* an accident, and how she killed
two birds with one stone or, to be more precise, killed one bird
and caged another with one shovel.

A week after Howard's conviction, Evelyn had the wild
trees topped or cut down (something Howard would never have
allowed), affording her a panoramic ocean view and giving the
knoll an expansive air.

She filed for divorce in April. Her most immediate concern
was a lack of income, but then she didn't have many expenses.
Stock dividends covered most of her needs, while her father
filled in the gap.

Samantha came home to visit every third weekend, and for
the two weeks before summer quarter began. When she went
back to school, Evelyn went shopping for a dog to keep her
company and found Lettie, another Shih Tzu.

The Evelyn Marsh Gallery and Gift Shop opened the last
week of June, and Brooke came to work for her. The storefront
was on the south side of State Street, just two blocks east of
The Whitfield Gallery. From the day the gallery opened, there
was brisk foot traffic. The originals were a hard sell, but it
didn't matter; the peripheral items — mugs, magnets, notepads,
placemats and coasters — outsold the paintings, and the giclée
prints sold well enough. There were plans for a book and a
calendar. Brooke manned the shop from Wednesday through
Sunday. Evelyn joined her most afternoons. It was good to
mingle with fans of her work. She stood behind the counter and
listened to the comments, which were mostly complimentary

and gave her a boost of confidence and a sense of accomplishment.

On a Saturday in September, a man strolled into the store who looked vaguely familiar. He wore a Hawaiian shirt in a muted leaf pattern, sunglasses, and a Panama hat. He poked around the tables and displays, picking up first one item, then another, clandestinely glancing from time to time at Evelyn. He stood with crossed arms and looked up at the originals on the wall. She couldn't place him in his current outfit, and it wasn't until he spoke that she realized who he was.

"I admire your work," Detective Olson said.

"Thank you, Detective."

"You can call me Bill."

"Bill. That's my father's name."

"I know. How have you been?"

"Keeping busy."

He gave her an odd, almost guilty look. "I've been in before, but you weren't here."

"I don't come in everyday. I have to have time to paint."

"Yes. You know, I've thought of you over the past months. You made an impression during the trial."

"How so?"

"It was a difficult time for you. You handled it with remarkable grace and composure."

"I didn't have any choice."

"And I love your paintings. They have a haunting quality, like questions unanswered."

He looked up and she followed his gaze. He was staring at the garden scene, and she realized with a shock that he was looking at the murder weapon right there beside her hat and trowel and gloves, the gloves she'd dropped into the beach basket. Not that he would notice, or put two and two together, but she steered him toward the suitcase painting that she'd entitled *Coming or Going?*

"Evelyn? Do you mind if I call you Evelyn?"

"That depends. Is this an official inquiry?"

"God forbid, no," he chuckled. "I hope you won't think this is inappropriate, considering how we met, but I was hoping you'd have lunch with me sometime, or coffee, or...whatever."

He seemed so hopeful that she was charmed. "Why not?" she said. It might be nice to have the company of an attentive male from time to time.

He bought a mug and coaster depicting a rowboat piled with fishing gear pulled up on a beach, and footprints in the sand leading off canvas to the right.

That evening she took the garden painting home and painted out the gloves. *You can never be too careful*, she thought.

On a cool autumn morning, with the scent of honeysuckle in the air, Evelyn knelt in the front garden, trowel in hand, weeding. She looked up at Lettie's growl and saw dirt pushing out of a hole. The dog trotted forward, barking at the mound, and started to dig with her front paws.

"No, Lettie, bad dog! Get away!" She reached out and pulled the dog back by the collar. "Sit!" she commanded.

The dog sat, growling softly. Evelyn went back to weeding. Sometime later, the mound began to grow as the gopher pushed more dirt from its tunnels. It was like watching a volcano grow. A small gopher peered over the rim. It retreated into its tunnel when Evelyn stood. She gathered a sheaf of weeds and left it at the entrance to the hole. "Eat up," she told the gopher; "there's plenty more where that came from." Then she knelt on the cool earth and scratched behind the dog's ears. The growl turned to a groan of contentment. "Sometimes," she said, "it's best to share our garden."

The sheaf of weeds shook, and a moment later the green shoots began disappearing down the hole.

Moss Beach, February 1st to September 1st, 2016

Made in the USA
San Bernardino, CA
21 August 2017